The Unknown Billionaire (Captured by Love Book 6)

Miranda P. Charles

Published by MPC Romance Publishing
Cover Art by Viola Estrella

ISBN-13: 978-1537583884
ISBN-10: 1537583883

http://www.mirandapcharles.com

The Unknown Billionaire (Captured by Love Book 6)

Books by Miranda P. Charles

Lifestyle by Design Series
Will To Love
Heart Robber
Ray of Love

Secret Dreams Series
Secret Words
Secret Designs
Secret Moves
Secret Tastes

Time for Love Series
Forever
Finally
Again
Always
At Last

Captured by Love
The Unwilling Executive
The Unyielding Bachelor
The Undercover Playboy
The Unintended Fiancé
The Unforgettable Ex
The Unknown Billionaire
The Unmasked CEO

CHAPTER ONE

"I'm betting on Jarryd."

Marilyn Grant frowned at the glowing Jade Renner-Bilton before nodding and calling up the Notes app on her phone. She opened the document where she recorded her friends' bets for their Captured by Love game and tapped J-A-R-R-Y-D next to Jade's name.

"Are you annoyed at me?" Jade asked in surprise.

She showed some teeth as she forced a smile. "No."

Jade stared at her, confused. "You don't want me to bet on Jarryd?"

"You can bet on anyone you want," she said with a despondent sigh, letting her mask slip.

"What's wrong?" Jade took her arm and led her to a wicker love seat on the patio by the back entrance of Rick and Lexie Donnelly's house, where their gang of close friends and select relatives were celebrating an engagement and four pregnancies, including Jade's.

Marilyn plonked herself next to Jade on the sofa. Good thing they were now out of earshot of their other buddies, most of whom were congregated in the expansive garden decked out with ample outdoor seating. Others were having a dip in the inviting swimming pool, enjoying the perfect Sydney weather on the second day of the Australian summer.

"I just don't want to imagine him winning our Captured by Love game, that's all," she answered Jade truthfully.

"Why not?"

She let out a big exhale. "I didn't want to tell anyone this because I don't want to make a big deal of it, but Jarryd and I dated for three weeks. Then two months ago, he dumped me."

Jade's mouth dropped open.

"Apparently, we don't have enough chemistry."

"That's what he told you?" Jade asked incredulously.

Marilyn nodded, glancing in Jarryd Westbourne's direction. Her heart galloped at the sight of him lounging casually as he chatted with the other guys, his dark brown eyes slightly squinting from the brightness of the afternoon sun. She'd been tempted to comment that his newly trimmed black hair suited him when they'd greeted each other earlier. But all they'd exchanged was a brief "hey, good to see you"—their first verbal conversation since Jarryd had told her two months ago that, while he found her attractive, he didn't think there was a spark between them.

Liar.

If there had been any more of a spark between them, they'd have spontaneously combusted.

Whatever his real reason, it sure as hell wasn't the flimsy excuse he'd given her. They'd *smouldered* together, damn it!

Marilyn shook her head vigorously to clear the hurtful thoughts from her head. Argh, she hated that her feelings for the man hadn't abated. Worse, seeing him today wearing a plain blue shirt that clung to his well-sculpted torso reminded her just how hot of a hunk he really was. And she so needed closure!

"Hey," Jade said softly, placing a hand on her arm.

"Do you know if Lucas has ever mentioned my parents to Jarryd, since your husband is his bestie among us?"

"I don't think so. Why?"

"Well, Jarryd has known from the beginning I'm well-off—having a big house and driving a luxury car—but I'm sure he thought that was due to me running a successful business brokerage firm. Two days after we had a conversation about my parents, he ditched me. So I don't think he'd known before that I'm the daughter of *the* Grants of Grant Ace Holdings. I mean, my name doesn't normally appear alongside Mum and Dad's in the media since my business is independent from Grant Ace, and Jarryd probably didn't have a reason to make the connection before."

"Oh, honey. I know you don't like parading the fact that you are Barry and Alice Grant's daughter, but what makes you think that that's Jarryd's reason for breaking up with you?"

"I spent days and nights wondering what went wrong or what I might have done to turn him off," she said glumly. "We were having such a great time getting to know each other, and it wasn't until I mentioned my parents—specifically that they own several shopping centres around the world—that he suddenly started acting distant. Then he ditched me soon after."

"Surely he doesn't have anything against your family's shopping centres?" Jade asked with a frown.

"I think he might have been intimidated."

"Intimidated? But why? It couldn't be because your parents are super rich. We have millionaires and billionaires within our circle and he seems comfortable with all of us. In any case, no one here makes a big deal about anyone's financial standing."

"Maybe for him, being friends with someone from a billionaire family and going out with that person are two different things," Marilyn said with hurt in her voice. "He's not the first guy I've dated who couldn't seem to handle that I'm the only child of one of the wealthiest couples in Australia. Once they knew, either they took advantage of the fact they were dating a Grant, or they started acting funny around me. It's like they suddenly believed being with me would be hard work, or that I'd be too high-maintenance, or that they have to give me extravagant things to please me. That really hurt! I've shown time and again I'm completely happy with the simple things, like walks in the park or eating takeaway as opposed to being wined and dined in five-star restaurants. I'm just another girl wanting to find her special someone."

Jade patted her knee sympathetically.

"You know what?" Marilyn said with a huff, letting herself rant away since only Jade could hear. "If Jarryd believes that we're not compatible simply because he's not at the same level of financial means as my family, then he can take a hike. I have not given him any reason to believe I care about how much he earns or what his net worth is. Does he think I'm a snooty bitch?"

Jade squeezed her hand. "No one who knows you will ever think that. And I'm sure Jarryd knows you well enough."

"So what's his problem, then? It's definitely got nothing to do with lack of chemistry, because we had that in spades. *Spades!* And if he really knows me well enough, then he should also know that I don't give a stuff that he doesn't have millions of dollars to his name. All I want is his love." Her face burned at her last statement.

"You love him?"

She shrugged, glancing at Jarryd again. "I was getting there."

"Oh, Marilyn. Well, maybe it is a money thing," Jade said tentatively. "You know how some men feel like they always have to be the breadwinner?"

"Yeah," she said sadly. "Thing is, I don't care about that. I know how hard he works in his business. So what if his income is still small at this time? His business is growing. He has to tighten his belt until his hard work bears fruit."

Jade sighed. "Please don't tell anyone what I'm about to tell you, because Lucas told me that Jarryd doesn't want anyone else to know."

"Okay."

"When Jarryd started hiring trucks and equipment from Bilton Machineries, he wasn't satisfied with the answers to the technical queries given by the BDM assigned to him. Lucas stepped in to iron things out and, since my husband is a mechanic at heart, he actually enjoyed answering Jarryd's long list of questions. That was how they became friends."

Marilyn nodded. That part she was aware of. The two men had gotten along like a house on fire. Lucas had even referred Jarryd to Natasha Garrett, another close friend of theirs, which had resulted in Garrett Electricals working on one of Jarryd's projects. In fact, it was because of Jarryd's friendship with Lucas and Natasha that Jarryd had become a regular attendee to their group's get-togethers in the last five months. Now, Jarryd was considered part of their gang. And Marilyn had no choice but to continue to socialise with him, especially since their brief affair was unknown to most of their friends.

"When they became close," Jade said, "Lucas told Jarryd that if he wanted to buy some of the machineries—which would be better for Jarryd's construction company in the long run—Lucas would be willing to give him extended payment terms with an interest rate lower than what's available elsewhere. Bilton Machineries offers that only to a select few. But Jarryd said he couldn't afford to buy. Apparently, one of his major clients went bankrupt and couldn't pay progress payments amounting to several hundred thousands. What was worse was he'd focused on that big project and held back on other ones, so he was really cash-strapped. I don't know where he's at right now, but I doubt he could have turned his fortunes around in a matter of months when construction projects take a long time to complete. So maybe he's a bit embarrassed about the state of his finance after knowing your parents are billionaires? Maybe it's a pride thing for him?"

Marilyn shook her head, wondering why Jarryd hadn't told her all of those things. She would have suggested cheaper dates when they were still going out, especially when Jarryd had insisted on paying most of the time.

Pfft. As if you're special enough to him that he'd reveal his deepest secrets and fears to you.

She sniffed.

Pity the feelings weren't mutual.

And that statement just felt like a bucketful of hogwash.

Argh!

"Jade, slap me."

"What?"

"Slap me."

"Why?"

"Because I'm being stupid," she said with a whine. "I want to believe that Jarryd still wants me but that something else that's totally fixable is holding him back. But whether his problem is chemistry or money or whatever else, the fact remains that he *doesn't* want to be with me. So give me a hard slap and tell me to wake up. *Please.*"

Jade patted her cheek instead. "For the record, I think that Jarryd still likes you a lot, judging from the glances he's been throwing at you all day. I vote for fixing what's holding him back."

Marilyn groaned. "You are so bad for my sanity. I bet it's the pregnancy hormones that're making you think like this."

"Probably," Jade said with a chuckle, rubbing her slightly swollen belly. "But I'm starting to change my mind about what a nice guy he is. If he thinks you're shallow and snobbish, then he's a poor judge of character."

She smiled at her friend's show of loyalty. "I'm just unlucky in love."

"Hey, don't say that! It'll happen for you soon enough."

She made a sad face. She was starting to worry that *the* one didn't exist for her. At twenty-eight, she'd been on plenty of dates, some of them with the most eligible bachelors in Australia. But the three times she'd thought the guy could be the one, she'd been left disappointed and heartbroken.

Why did love keep on eluding her?

"You know," Jade said, "I do find it weird that after being infatuated with you like a lovesick puppy, Jarryd would suddenly change his mind after three short weeks, especially since you said you were getting along just fine. So how about I get Lucas to do some interrogating? Seeing that Lucas is his bestie in our group, he just might tell him something."

Marilyn nodded, liking that idea. She was tired of being in limbo, shackled there by her feelings for Jarryd and the belief that his reason for breaking up with her was nothing but a smokescreen to hide something he wanted to keep hidden. With only three weeks left before Christmas, she at least wanted to have some sort of clarity so she wouldn't spend the coming holidays thinking of nothing but him.

"Can you ask Lucas now?" she pleaded with Jade.

*****

Jarryd Westbourne scanned Rick and Lexie's large yard, seeing the happy faces of friends as well as those of a handful of people he'd just met today. But where was Marilyn? He leaned back on his seat, glancing around.

Ah, there she was on the patio, frowning at her phone. She was probably attending to something important to be sitting there by herself. Anyway, it was good she wasn't near him. The farther she was, the easier for him not to stare.

He forced himself to avert his gaze, shaking his head for wanting to keep on gawking. But could he really blame himself? He hadn't seen her in two months and she looked absolutely beautiful today, with her layered shoulder-length blond hair dancing in the gentle breeze. And, heck, she was downright sexy in that green sundress that almost matched the colour of her eyes, her lithe figure showing every time a gust of wind wrapped the soft material of her outfit around her.

Maybe if he hadn't been missing her so badly, he wouldn't be—

Oh, for fuck's sake, why couldn't he stop himself from pining for her? He was thirty-one, not fifteen!

"Hey, dude."

He looked behind him with a start.

"Hey," he said to Lucas, who had a funny smirk on his face.

"Talk to you for a sec?"

"Sure."

"So what's this I've been hearing about you and Marilyn?" Lucas said in a low voice as they walked towards the perimeter of the garden.

Jarryd glanced at his buddy sharply. "What have you been hearing?"

"That you slept with her, then dumped her."

Heat rose to his face, his jaw slackening.

"So what happened?" Lucas asked. "You couldn't wait to go out with her before. Even today, you can't take your eyes off her."

He ran his fingers through his hair, glancing back to ensure no one was following them. "*Dumped* is a harsh word. It was more like I thought it wasn't going to work out."

"And why wasn't it going to work out?"

"Because…" Damn. What excuse could he give? "It hit me that we were going way too fast towards a serious relationship and that scared me," he said with enough gravity to sound convincing.

"Really? I thought you were already falling fast for her even before she agreed to go out with you."

Jarryd flushed, but kept an impassive face. "Obviously not. Anyway, who told you?"

"My wife. She's been talking to Marilyn. Apparently, Marilyn doesn't buy your reason for breaking up with her."

He pressed his lips into a thin line, not at all surprised by that.

He'd actually meant to say there was *not enough* spark between them, but for some reason he'd ended up saying they had none—probably from his agitation at having to end things with her. The hurt and bewilderment on Marilyn's face had stopped him from correcting himself, lest he make things worse by inadvertently giving away too much. In any case, all he'd succeeded in doing was sounding like a heartless liar.

"What exactly did you tell her?" Lucas prodded.

Jarryd's phone rang, saving him from answering Lucas. "Sorry, it's my lawyer. I have to get this."

"Sure. We'll continue this later." Lucas clapped his shoulder before walking away.

"Hello, Carl," he greeted after Lucas was out of hearing distance.

"Hello, Jarryd. Is this a good time to talk?" asked Carl Peters.

"Yes, I'm just at a party."

"Oh. Is Marilyn Grant there?"

"Yes."

"I'm surprised you risked being in the same place as her."

He sighed. He knew he shouldn't have come today. But these people were his friends, even though they had no knowledge of the drama happening in his life. Besides, he'd missed them, especially Marilyn.

"Anyway, I have some good news for you," Carl said. "Probably great timing since you're there with Marilyn."

Jarryd straightened. "Uh-huh."

"Bray Hayden, my PI, managed to find out that Barry and Alice Grant have never met with Patrick O'Neill about appearing on *Biz Q&A*. There was no need for a meeting because both of them declined the written invitation to appear on the show."

His heart raced in excitement. "And Bray is certain that the Grants and Patrick are not connected in any other way?"

"Yes. Apparently, Patrick is keen to have high-profile billionaires like Alice and Barry to be guest mentors on his show. But the Grants are not friends with Patrick. It appears they haven't even met in person."

Sheer relief washed over Jarryd. Thank God for that. "Do you know when Patrick plans to formally challenge the will's validity?" he asked.

"He's still holding off on it. But that doesn't mean he won't ever do it. What did he call you two months ago when he stormed into your office?"

"A scheming thief and evil manipulator," Jarryd said dryly. "I still find it strange that he waited seven months before claiming I manipulated Margaret into writing a new will for my benefit."

"Well, his lawyer said he'd been too shocked and grief-stricken to do anything those first seven months since Margaret's death. Apparently, Patrick was supposed to be in California with Margaret when Margaret slipped and hit her head on those blasted marble stairs. He'd felt guilty about not being with her."

Sadness hit Jarryd at the memory of his birth mother, whom he'd met for the first time less than two years ago. When he'd received a call from her out of the blue, asking if he'd want to connect, he'd been shocked. Apparently, Margaret had wanted to find him for a long time, but had been waiting for him to instigate the connection—until she hadn't wanted to wait any longer.

He hadn't hesitated agreeing to meet her. He'd already toyed with the idea of searching for his birth mother, with the encouragement of his wonderful adoptive parents. But the last thing he'd expected was to come face-to-face with *the* Margaret O'Neill, widow of Harold Greeves—the business genius who'd steered Greeves

Minerals Corp into becoming one of the world's biggest miners of diamonds and other gemstones.

Five years ago, Margaret's grieving face had been all over the news when her billionaire husband and their son—their only child together—had died from injuries sustained in a car accident in Germany.

The spotlight had been on Margaret again three years ago, when she'd married Patrick O'Neill, the charismatic and popular head panellist of the respected TV show *Biz Q&A*. The man who, two months ago, had vowed to make Jarryd's life hell for Jarryd's supposed manipulation of Margaret.

"Don't worry, Jarryd," Carl was saying, dragging his attention back to their conversation. "If Patrick makes any legal or public accusation that you coerced Margaret into giving you the bulk of her estate, we'll pull out all the stops to prove that he only wants to ruin your character so he can end up with Margaret's money. Besides, he might have the adulation of his fans and the support of some very influential people, but you have the money to fight him on this. You're the billionaire, Jarryd. *You*."

"Well, I don't plan to live like one until all the question marks on my character are gone. And I can only hope that Patrick will give due respect to his departed wife by not publicising any of this."

"I hope so too," Carl said. "But personally, I don't think we have to worry about Patrick bringing this out in the public arena until he's sure he can win. And right now, he knows he can't. He has no proof. But he'd want to protect his image to the fullest, so he wouldn't want people to know that his wife decided to leave most of her wealth to a son that she'd never told him about."

Jarryd ran a hand over his face. Even he had been stunned to learn of his inheritance. Margaret had never told him about it.

What made it worse was that, apart from his parents, he hadn't told anyone about meeting his birth mother either. Margaret had requested that they keep their reunion a secret for a short period so they could get to know each other without the unwanted attention that might arise from Margaret's public profile as CEO of Greeves Minerals. Then Margaret had asked him to continue keeping their relationship a secret when Greeves Minerals started negotiations to buy Well of Brilliance, a diamond retail company and custom jewellery maker that Margaret had been especially keen on acquiring. She'd been concerned that juicy news about her personal life might result in negative publicity that could affect their success.

Now that Margaret was gone, he was still duty-bound to hide his relationship with her. Olivia Greeves, Margaret's sister-in-law who was now Greeves Minerals' CEO, was trying to get the negotiations back on track to acquire Well of Brilliance. Olivia, too, had asked Jarryd to stay quiet until the Well of Brilliance deal was finalised. The talks had been going on and off for far too long, and Olivia didn't want anything that might stall it again. Of course he'd agreed. He now owned fifty percent of Greeves Minerals and wanted what was best for the company.

He shook his head to clear it. "Anyway, Carl, is there anything else you wanted to talk to me about?"

"That's it for now. Have you spoken to Marilyn today?"

Carl's sudden change of topic made Jarryd's breath hitch. "I'm just about to. Apparently, she wants to know exactly why I broke up with her. You have no idea how relieved I am to know that her parents aren't connected with Patrick."

"But hasn't Olivia asked you to stay quiet about your relationship with Margaret?"

"Yes, for now. I don't have to mention Margaret to anyone. I've managed to keep it to myself for all these months."

"Well, good luck with Marilyn today."

"Thanks," he said before they said their goodbyes.

Jarryd took a minute to compose himself after hanging up.

If only he hadn't been so muddled two months ago.

But he'd been taken aback by Patrick O'Neill suddenly accusing him of something so unthinkable as coercing his birth mother into writing a new will so he'd get the bulk of Margaret's billion-dollar estate. Patrick was an influential, well-known and well-respected man. Jarryd knew that plenty of people would believe Patrick's words without a question, while there Jarryd was, a nobody who'd suddenly become a billionaire after the death of Margaret O'Neill—who'd never told anyone she had a living son she'd given up for adoption, much less that she'd found him.

He still couldn't believe the timing. He'd been succeeding at warding off his disquiet at Patrick's accusations by being in Marilyn's arms, when Marilyn had informed him that her parents were Barry and Alice Grant of Grant Ace.

He snickered dryly, remembering how he couldn't wait to ask Carl to find out if the Grants were acquainted with Patrick, and how he'd just stared into space for minutes when Carl's PI had informed him that Barry and Alice were being asked by Patrick to appear on several episodes of *Biz Q&A*.

He'd still made the right decision breaking up with Marilyn then, right?

Knowing what he knew then, yes. He'd assumed that the Grants and Patrick were well acquainted and he'd wanted to protect Marilyn and her parents from any negative publicity that could fall on them because of his conflict with Patrick.

But now he would have done things differently. He would have fully prepared himself for a let-her-down-gently breakup instead of refusing to think about it and only blurting out the words when he was already in front of her.

Now the coast was somewhat clear again, and he couldn't wait to smooth things out with her. But how would he start wooing her again after he'd used the wrong fucking words?

No spark between them.

Seriously, he was an idiot.

CHAPTER TWO

Marilyn's heart skipped before banging hard in her chest. Jarryd was walking towards the patio. What had Lucas told him?

She swallowed, marshalling her courage. "Why, hello there, stranger," she called out, keen to pretend she was in no way affected by his proximity.

Jarryd smiled back, making her heart race faster.

He stopped in front of her, his chest heaving from his deep inhalation as he eyed the vacant space in the two-seater couch. He seemed to be hesitating.

Her excitement disappeared in a flash. Damn him. Couldn't he make it less obvious that he didn't want to be close to her?

"You don't have to sit next to me if you don't want to," she said, meaning to sound teasing but hearing the hurt in her own voice.

"Marilyn," Jarryd said, his tone chiding.

"What?" she asked, arching an eyebrow.

"Don't say it like you think I have something against sitting next to you."

She gave him a saccharine-sweet smile. "Well, you do, don't you? Don't worry. You won't burn yourself. There's no spark between us, remember?" Ugh, what the hell was wrong with her? Did she really need to pick at that wound right now?

Jarryd's lips curved into a semblance of a smile as he proceeded to sit next to her on the love seat, his fingers grazing her knee as he settled himself.

Zap.

Startled, she glanced up at Jarryd.

His eyes were round, probably as much as hers were.

"Sorry," Jarryd said, his voice croaking. "Must be some static."

"Yeah, what else could it be?" she asked tightly.

Jarryd sighed. "Lucas said you've been wondering about my real reason for ending things between us. I thought I'd explain."

She sat up straight and fixed her gaze up ahead. No way would she look like a yearning mess of a woman who was missing him terribly—even if she was that.

Silence.

"Look," she said, giving Jarryd a small smile. "I don't have a problem with you ending things between us. I'm not someone who'd force a person to be with me against their will. My problem is I can't relax about something when I think I haven't been given everything I need to know. And what you told me as your reason for not wanting to see me anymore just struck me as being untrue."

Oh God. She hoped she didn't sound like an egotist who couldn't believe that a guy had ditched her.

Jarryd stood up and went to the nearby chair.

Her eyes smarted. Was he really that uncomfortable with her now?

But her breath caught when Jarryd dragged the chair so he was facing her fully.

"Marilyn," Jarryd said as he sat down, holding her gaze. "Two months ago I was totally muddled. Someone close to me died nine months ago, and complications had arisen because of that. I was having a hell of a time with personal problems."

Her brows furrowed in concern. "Died? Who?"

"A... relative. I didn't tell you because I didn't want to involve you in the mess. Like I said, I was totally muddled back then."

"Are you okay now?"

"Things aren't fully sorted, but yes, I'm okay now."

She stared at Jarryd, her heart constricting. So he'd been grieving and he hadn't needed her comfort? He'd had a difficult problem and he hadn't wanted to share it with her? That said a lot.

"I didn't mean what I said when I broke up with you," Jarryd said.

She frowned. "Which bit? That we have no spark?"

Jarryd nodded eagerly. "Yes! I didn't mean to say that."

"And yet you did."

"Like I said, I was totally muddled."

"So what did you mean to say?"

"Well, I actually meant to say that we didn't have *enough* spark. But I wouldn't have meant that either."

She shook her head to clear her confusion. "What?"

"We have extraordinary chemistry, Marilyn. That can't be denied." Jarryd looked down to the ground. "But I needed to pour a lot of time and energy into my issues, plus I didn't want to involve you in them. So with everything I was going through, I thought it was best not to continue with our relationship."

She took a deep breath. Okay, right. Not ready for a relationship. That she understood. How many times had she used that same excuse with some of the men she'd dated after she'd discovered she didn't want something long-term with them?

But she had to know something else. "Did my parents have anything to do with your decision?"

Jarryd looked at her sharply. "What do you mean?"

"I have a feeling you weren't impressed by the fact that I'm the daughter of Barry and Alice Grant of Grant Ace. I thought you might have been... well... intimidated by them being so rich."

Jarryd's brows furrowed. "No. I *was* surprised when you told me who they were, but I'm actually impressed. Not by them being rich, but with you not using your parents to get ahead in your business. I bet not many of your clients know who your parents are."

"I see," she murmured, her chest compressing further. There it went—the final sliver of hope she'd been hanging on to. Clearly and plainly, Jarryd just didn't see her as someone he could share deeper and more meaningful things with.

She nodded, finally accepting it. For Jarryd, all they'd had was a strong physical attraction. They might have had extraordinary chemistry—still did, if her body's reaction to his closeness was anything to go by—but it was still only physical.

The feelings weren't mutual, after all.

Marilyn squared her shoulders and rose to her feet. She'd had to break a few men's hearts in the past herself. She could understand Jarryd, even if he was hurting her.

"Thank you for explaining things to me," she said with a smile as she smoothed her dress. "Anyway, I'm feeling a bit hungry. I'm gonna go get something. See you later."

She hurried away from him and made a beeline for the dessert table. Something sweet should make her feel better, shouldn't it?

She stared at the different cakes on offer, forcing herself to ignore the ache in her chest. She wasn't going to show him how much she was hurting.

"Can't decide?" a voice said next to her.

She smiled at Simon Alexander. "They all look so tempting."

Simon leaned close to whisper in her ear. "I have it on good authority that Jarryd likes chocolate mud cake. I'm sure he'd be over the moon if you spoon-fed him some on that love seat."

She frowned at him. "Have you been speaking to Lucas?"

"Hey, everybody knows that Jarryd's got the hots for you. So he finally 'fessed up, huh? He's done nothing but look at you all day."

Marilyn rolled her eyes. What bad timing for people to be bringing up this Jarryd's-got-the-hots-for-you crap. "Turns out I'm not ideal girlfriend material."

"What?" Simon asked in shock.

She shook her head, trying to look nonchalant. But her expression must have betrayed her, because Simon was now inspecting her face.

"Hey, it's cool," she said. "A person can be physically attracted to someone, but not be interested enough to want a relationship with them. It happens. It's not a crime. I've been guilty of the same thing in the past."

"Was he asking you for a no-strings affair back there?" Simon gestured to the patio.

"No," she scoffed. "Can we talk about this later? Now's not a good time."

"Sorry," Simon said, putting an arm around her and giving her a sympathetic squeeze. "I didn't mean to be nosy. Want me to be your date for the rest of the day and keep him away?"

She dipped her head onto his shoulder. Simon was her best male friend whom she'd known for over ten years. A few years back, before Simon had decided he much preferred the bachelor lifestyle, they'd tried dating for real. But when it came to trying to sleep together, they'd ended up laughing so hard at their attempt to end up in bed that they'd given up then and there. Much as they adored each other, they simply didn't have that physical chemistry.

"I doubt you'd need to keep him away," she said with a little sniff. "I bet he's the one who's going to keep on avoiding me, not the other way around."

"Hey, it's his loss. Anyway, let's change the subject. Have you decided on whether to go on *Biz Q&A* or not?"

"Not yet," she said, picking a strawberry and nibbling on it. Jarryd wasn't a big fan of strawberries. So there must really be something wrong with the man to give her up, right? Hah!

"It'll be great for your charitable works," Simon said as he led her towards one of the several outdoor seats.

"I've thought about that. I'm still surprised that Patrick contacted me personally after my parents declined the offer. I don't like being in the spotlight, as you know, but I get that it's about helping the young entrepreneurs who go on it. And, yes, I suppose I could mention some of my charity fundraising events and lift their profiles."

"Starting with our Captured by Love game," Simon said with a laugh. "Imagine asking people from all over Australia—the world, even—to bet on which bachelor will be the next to get stupid and give up their freedom."

Marilyn chuckled. "Don't give me ideas, because I'm liking the thought of taking this game to another level. And when I do, I'm gonna campaign so hard for everyone to bet on you," she said, wagging her finger at Simon. "There'll be so much pressure that even *you* will have to seriously consider finding a nice girl to fall in love with."

Simon snorted. "I'm not susceptible to that kind of pressure."

She sighed. "I wish I could go back to not caring about finding someone special. I don't know why I'm so intent on finding my soulmate all of a sudden." Her gaze involuntarily went to the patio. Jarryd was no longer there. Against her will, she searched the yard for him and found him sitting with a bunch of others near the outdoor bar. She caught him watching her and Simon, before immediately averting his gaze.

"I've never known you to be such a quitter," Simon quipped.

She frowned at him. "Excuse me?"

"You heard me," Simon said unapologetically.

She saw her scowling image reflected in the lenses of Simon's dark sunglasses. "And what would you have me do? Force myself on someone who doesn't want a relationship with me?"

"But he's still attracted to you, right? So what's wrong with no-strings? You've done that a few times in the past. And it's not like you're in that much of a hurry to get hitched, are you?"

"I don't know if he's *still* attracted to me right now," Marilyn said with a pout.

"That he can't make himself stop looking at you tells me a different story."

"Is he looking this way again?"

"Yeah," Simon said with a chuckle. "Like he doesn't want to but can't help himself."

Too bad she'd left her sunnies on the coffee table on the patio. She, too, would love to watch Jarryd without being obvious about it.

"I think he still has a huge crush on you."

"You think?" she asked in a pathetic voice.

"Maybe Jarryd's just the type who thinks he might be insulting you with a suggestion of booty calls. Have you considered a casual fling for the time being?"

"No. I should have spoken to you earlier, Mr. Playboy," she said with playful sarcasm. "Only you would suggest something like that to me."

Simon laughed. "Tell me again why I never got to show you how good *I* am in bed."

It was Marilyn's turn to laugh out loud. "Because this was what we ended up doing whenever we tried to have sex." She pointed to herself, chortling.

"Yeah," Simon said with a wide grin. "So what's stopping you from telling Jarryd you're okay with no-commitment fun? Snare him the sneaky way, I say."

She let out a long breath. "I don't know."

"Think about it while I get a drink. Want me to get you one since Jarryd's sitting right next to the fridge?"

She shook her head. "I'll join you over there after I go to the bathroom. Might as well prove to Jarryd I'm okay with being around him."

Simon snickered before heading off.

She chewed her lip as she walked towards the house. Would she really consider a casual relationship with Jarryd?

Well, didn't some long-term relationships start out as sex-only affairs? She only needed to look at some of her happily-in-love friends to know that was true.

Her brain traitorously reminded her of her hot days and nights with Jarryd. Oh, she'd had the strongest orgasms of her life with him. "I don't mind booty calls as long as they're from Jarryd," she mumbled to herself.

Problem was, from what Marilyn could gather from their brief chat, her being hurt further had a much higher probability of happening than Jarryd falling for her. Would she really be so stupid as to put herself in a hurtful, embarrassing situation when Jarryd had already given her everything she needed to have closure and move on?

CHAPTER THREE

Jarryd tried not to glare at Simon as the guy joined their table. Instead, he took a swig of his beer to push down the jealousy that was churning within him.

What was with that hug Simon had given Marilyn? He knew the two had been good friends for years, but this was the first time he'd seen them in an embrace that wasn't meant to be a hello or goodbye. It had been too sweet for his liking.

Had Marilyn gone to Simon for comfort after he'd stuffed up yet again? Worse, it appeared Simon had truly lifted Marilyn's spirits, with her laughter looking genuine from where he sat.

He took another big gulp of his drink. He should have thought about what he was going to say first before he'd tried to explain himself. Their conversation had headed the wrong way, and now all Marilyn understood was that he wasn't ready for a relationship.

Served him right for being unprepared. Yet again.

They'd need to have a heart-to-heart talk. Well, as heart-to-heart as he could manage without mentioning Margaret and Patrick O'Neill. Unfortunately, they were at a party—unless they went to an empty room inside the house and locked themselves in.

Jarryd sighed as his body reacted to his idea. He missed making love to her, missed kissing her, missed holding her against him. He simply missed *her*.

He kept one eye on the house to watch for Marilyn while he listened to the other guys talk about the football game last night. Eventually she came out the back door and headed for their table.

His heart thudded and his cock jerked. He hoped she'd take the empty seat between him and Simon.

But Marilyn went straight for the fridge near him, and Simon was quick to be by her side.

Argh, he should have been faster. What was wrong with him?

"What would you like?" Simon asked Marilyn.

"Just cold sparkling water. I'm parched," she said with a smile.

Simon grabbed a large bottle of Evian and poured her a glass. "Feeling better?" he asked as he handed it to her.

Marilyn nodded.

"How about a movie tonight to cheer you up?" Simon asked softly.

Jarryd frowned. He didn't like the sound of that.

"Um," Marilyn murmured, gazing at Simon.

Jarryd tried not to stare, but the two were right there in his line of sight. And he had to restrain himself from rising to his feet and slapping Simon's hand that was running up and down Marilyn's arm. Why the hell was Simon now flirting with her?

"You know what I'm talking about, Marilyn," Simon was saying in a soft tone that Jarryd had to strain to hear. "No pressure. No strings. Just two friends having a fun time together."

What? And why the hell was Marilyn grinning? Was she enjoying Simon's proposition? Marilyn, of all people, would know what a big playboy Simon was. Surely, she wasn't entertaining the thought of sleeping with one of her best friends?

Why not? They care about each other.

Ah, hell. He couldn't believe this was happening.

"You don't need to answer me yet," Simon said. "Tell me before the end of the day what you decide, okay?"

"Okay."

Jarryd heard the laughter in Marilyn's voice when she answered.

Fuck.

Simon pulled out a chair for Marilyn—the one Jarryd had hoped she'd take. At least that was something. It gave him an opportunity to stop Simon from hogging Marilyn's attention.

"Hey, guys," Rick said, approaching their table and holding something in his large hands. "I've got something to show you."

"What is it?" Marilyn asked.

Rick grinned and placed whatever it was on the table.

A small black thing with a long tail scurried towards Marilyn's direction.

"No!" she shrieked, springing from her seat. The mouse was running so fast that it fell off the table and landed near her feet.

Marilyn jumped on Simon's lap, clinging to his shirt as she lifted her feet off the ground in fear.

Jarryd's instant jealousy at her action was overshadowed by his concern for her. "Hey, dude, that's not cool," he said, glaring at Rick.

"It's only a toy," Rick said with a laugh. "I was telling the others about how lifelike it looks and I thought I'd try it on you guys."

"Don't you know Marilyn's phobic of those things?" Jarryd asked, scowling as he noticed Simon's arms around Marilyn.

Rick's face fell. "I didn't know. Sorry, Marilyn. It's only a toy."

"Hey, it's only a toy," Simon repeated against Marilyn's hair, rubbing her back soothingly.

Jarryd hated what he was seeing, but he was worried enough about Marilyn not to look away. She seemed to be calming down, her breathing no longer fast and shallow.

He knew just how much mice and rats frightened her. Once, he'd taken her to an old terrace his company was refurbishing, and she'd screamed in terror when two big rodents had run across them in the empty building. It had taken her a while to calm back down.

He totally understood her phobia. In one of her first overseas travels for her charitable works in third-world countries, she'd witnessed several rats gnawing at a dying man's sore-covered feet. She and the medical team who'd made the trip to the man's shack had been too late. She'd told him the poor guy had died in front of them a few minutes later.

The event had traumatised her, bringing on her loathing for the vermin, and heightening her passion for charity fundraising.

"I'm okay," Marilyn said shakily, getting out of Simon's lap and moving back to her seat. She was flushed, and Jarryd was sure it was both from being scared and from being embarrassed.

He reached out to touch her arm.

Marilyn smiled at him—a sweet, grateful smile that lifted his hopes.

Their eye contact was broken by the other guests rushing to them.

"What happened?" Lexie asked.

Rick told them.

Lexie gasped, giving her husband's bicep a slap. "She hates mice with a passion."

"I didn't know," Rick said, his tone full of apology.

"No worries, Rick. I'm fine," Marilyn said with a weak laugh. "Nothing to see here, guys."

Simon offered Marilyn a glass of water and placed a loose arm around her shoulders.

Jarryd's jealousy returned with force. There was no way he'd let Marilyn take up Simon's offer of casual sex. If he had his way, she wouldn't even be considering it.

He hid a sigh of relief when Simon finally took his arm from around Marilyn. Not about to let an opportunity pass him by, he leaned over to whisper in her ear. "Are you okay?"

"Yes, thank you."

"Hey, I was wondering if we can continue the conversation we were having at the patio earlier? There's more that I wanted to tell you."

"Oh? I thought we were finished."

"I wasn't," he said softly, pleading to her with his eyes.

"Oka-ay," Marilyn said slowly. "Shall we go over there, then?" She pointed to the quiet spot where she and Simon had had their earlier chat.

"Actually, I was thinking it might be better if we do it after the party. How about we go to dinner so we can have a proper talk? I can pick you up from your place if you want to go home first, or we can go straight from here."

Marilyn stared at him and he held his breath. Had he pushed it too far with the dinner thing?

"Okay," she finally said. "I'd like to go home and get changed first. Pick me up at seven?"

"Yes, perfect."

He sat back on his chair with a smile. Marilyn wouldn't be going home with Simon tonight.

And he was having a date with her.

*****

Jarryd rang Marilyn's doorbell, his heart seeming to race a thousand beats a minute. He was more nervous now than he'd been on their very first date.

He glanced down at the bunch of flowers he was holding, hoping Marilyn wouldn't find him too presumptuous. But he wanted to be clear that he intended for this to be a romantic date, that he wanted to pick up where they'd left off—if she'd allow it.

The door opened and Marilyn's mouth hung open as she took in the beautiful bouquet made up of roses, lilies and mini-carnations.

"Hi," he said.

"Hi." She opened the door wider to let him in.

"These are, of course, for you." He handed her the bunch as he leaned down to kiss her cheek.

"Thank you. Um, unfortunately, we can't leave yet," she said in a low voice. "My mum turned up unannounced five minutes ago to talk to me about something. But I told her I'm going out to dinner, so she won't be staying long."

Jarryd's breathing shallowed as he heard footsteps coming from further inside. Last thing he expected was to meet Alice Grant tonight. "How about I come back later? You can call me when you're ready to go."

"Oh, no need for that," a beautiful older woman said, appearing with a friendly smile directed at him. Her gaze flickered to the flowers Marilyn was holding, then back to him. "I'm Alice, Marilyn's mother," she said, gesturing for a handshake.

"It's a pleasure to meet you, Mrs. Grant," he said, quick to take the proffered hand of the woman who was a carbon copy of Marilyn, but a few years older. "I'm Jarryd Westbourne."

"Happy to meet you, Jarryd. I should have called Marilyn before I turned up. I just assumed she wouldn't be going out tonight after just having been to a pool party. Four of her friends celebrated their pregnancies, and apparently one couple also got engaged today."

"Jarryd knows, Mum," Marilyn said with a laugh. "He was at the same party. He's the newest member of our gang."

"Oh, I see." Alice looked pleased. "Well, I won't stay long. You don't mind if I finish my drink, do you?"

"Of course not, Mrs. Grant," he answered, with Marilyn echoing him.

He followed the two women to the back of the house, with Alice commenting on how pretty the flowers were. No doubt Alice was thinking he was wooing Marilyn, if not that he was her boyfriend already.

And Marilyn hadn't said anything to correct whatever wrong assumption her mother might be making. That was a good sign. A very good sign that excited him. This evening had started off well, especially since Alice seemed to be the friendly, welcoming type.

"Can I get you a drink, Jarryd?" Marilyn asked.

"Are you having anything?"

"I'm having iced tea with Mum."

"I'll have the same, thanks."

Marilyn walked to the inviting kitchen, which was in the same room as the open-plan informal living area they were in.

"So, Jarryd," Alice said, settling down on a leather chair and motioning for him to take a seat on the couch. "You're part of that group of friends that include Rick and Lexie?"

"Yes. Lucas was the one who introduced me to the gang. Our friendship developed after I became a client of Bilton Machineries."

"Oh, what do you do?"

"I run a construction company."

"Which one?"

"It's called Westbourne Constructions. It's still relatively small, so you probably haven't heard of it."

Alice nodded her head. "How did you get into that business? And is it what you've always wanted to do?"

"I enjoy it enough. I started out as an apprentice carpenter when I was in my teens. Over time, I became a project manager for the company I used to work for. When my boss retired and sold the company, I decided to open my own business. I was lucky to have some of our regular clients follow me."

Alice asked him a few more questions, including where he lived and how his parents were. He answered them honestly, careful to give only the details that wouldn't lead to revealing his relationship with Margaret O'Neill and his conflict with Patrick.

"Done with your interrogation, Mum?" Marilyn asked dryly as she rejoined them, handing him a glass of iced tea and sitting beside him.

Alice chuckled. "I just wanted to get to know Jarryd at little bit. But, okay, I'll take the hint and leave you kids alone so you can go on your date. I'll have that talk with you some other time, Marilyn. Maybe tomorrow?"

"Sure, Mum."

Jarryd stood up when Alice got out of her chair.

"I'm so glad to have met you, Jarryd," Alice said, giving him a kiss goodbye on both cheeks. "I hope to see you again soon. Come with Marilyn to our house sometime."

"The pleasure's all mine, Mrs. Grant. And, thank you for the invitation. I appreciate it."

While Marilyn walked her mother to the door, Jarryd stayed behind in the lounge room, feeling quite pleased with himself. He seemed to have gotten Alice Grant's tick of approval as her daughter's date, even though the woman had been mistaken about the status of his relationship with Marilyn.

Of course, it wasn't her mother he was trying to impress. It was Marilyn herself. And he was pleasantly surprised that she still hadn't tried to correct Alice's evident assumption that they were going out. Was Marilyn open to getting back together with him too? His heart swelled at the thought.

If only he didn't need to hide certain things from her, then he'd feel more confident of tonight's outcome. Hopefully, it would only be a matter of weeks rather than months before the Tramwells accepted Greeves Minerals' offer for Well of Brilliance. Then he'd be free to talk about Margaret and the unexpected developments in his life.

He filled his lungs with air. Surely, Marilyn would understand why he had to keep things from her?

CHAPTER FOUR

"He seems like a nice guy."

Marilyn sighed, mentally berating herself for not clarifying the situation earlier. "He's just a friend, Mum, and we're just going out to dinner."

Her mother would want nothing more than to find her in a serious relationship. In fact, Alice had tried to set her up with eligible men more times than any other person in the last three years. Marilyn had had to put her foot down and tell her mother to stop or she'd never again take a guy home to meet her parents.

"Just a friend?" Alice said with scepticism as she opened the front door. "Bringing you flowers and not setting me straight when I assumed you're going out on a date?"

"He was probably just too polite to correct you."

"I didn't hear you try to correct me either."

She blushed. "Anyway, Mum, I can have dinner with you and Dad tomorrow. Then we can talk about what you wanted to talk about."

Alice grinned. "I see that you like this one a lot. Don't worry. I won't be all over him."

"You've already invited him to your house," Marilyn said with an eye-roll, although she was secretly pleased that her mother approved of Jarryd. That was one less thing she had to worry about *if* she and Jarryd ended up back together.

"Well, I know your friends. If he's accepted in that circle then I'm sure he's a good guy. Anyway, your dad and I are not free for dinner tomorrow. How about next Saturday?"

"Okay, then."

"And why don't you bring Jarryd along?"

"No," she said, horrified at the thought. Jarryd would run for the hills. Hadn't he broken up with her because he wasn't ready for a relationship? While she'd already guessed that Jarryd meant something romantic with the beautiful bouquet, she wasn't taking it as a given. For all she knew, Simon's joking invitation earlier for no-strings sex had encouraged Jarryd to consider the same thing, and that might be all he wanted from her.

"Fine," Alice said with disappointment. "Next time, maybe."

"I thought you wanted to talk about business and not socialise with my friends," Marilyn said dryly.

"Yes," Alice said in a low voice. "I might as well tell you now so you can start thinking about it. Your dad and I want to make a bid for Well of Brilliance. We only just found out that Lorna and Ben Tramwell are happy to sell. We think this is the right time to diversify further, and Well of Brilliance is the right company. But we want you to be on board."

"What do you mean?"

"If we're successful in our bid, then we're thinking it would be good if you could head Well of Brilliance. We think you'd love it."

Marilyn stared at her mother.

"We need to make a move soon," Alice said. "We believe they're close to considering Greeves Minerals' offer."

"Greeves Minerals? Is that why you declined to go on *Biz Q&A*? Doesn't Patrick now own part of that company?"

"Well, we assume he's inherited Margaret O'Neill's shares. But no, we didn't decline because of that. We just don't have the time to be on the show. But if you do decide to go on *Biz Q&A*, I agree that you should tell Patrick about Grant Ace bidding for Well of Brilliance. I'm sure Patrick won't have a problem with it, though. We're all professionals. Mind you, if we succeed in buying Well of Brilliance, appearing on *Biz Q&A* to announce our new venture would be a great idea."

"I'll have to think about it, Mum. I mean, I run my own business—"

"I know, darling," Alice interrupted with a hand on her arm. "You're doing very well with it and you have no idea how proud your dad and I are of you. But it's not as if business brokering is your passion, is it? You only went on your own because you wanted to prove to yourself and to everyone else that you're just not a pretty face who happens to have us as your parents, right?"

Marilyn's lips curved in acknowledgement. There had been a time when she had hated working for Grant Ace. She'd felt that their employees, especially the upper-level managers, had never believed her suitable for a management position.

Well, she herself had questioned if she was any good. She knew she'd leapfrogged her way up only because she was the bosses' daughter. Sure, she was entitled to it. After all, she expected to inherit the company eventually. But she'd constantly wondered if she could go far on her own. So she'd set out to find the answers by distancing herself from her parents, business-wise.

"You're an asset to any business, Marilyn. Your dad and I would be fools not to try to encourage you to rejoin our management team."

"Let me think about it, Mum," she said, even as her heart expanded from her mother's words.

"Of course. We'll see you next Saturday for dinner."

She gave Alice a kiss. "Drive safely and give my love to Dad."

Alice nodded, waving goodbye, and Marilyn shut the door.

Now she could go back to Jarryd.

She took a deep breath, putting aside her business conversation with her mother to concentrate on the man waiting for her in her living room. She found him sipping on his iced tea, reading a business magazine that she'd left on the coffee table.

Her breath hitched. She missed this—seeing Jarryd in her space. He'd always looked like he belonged here. Or rather, like he belonged *with her*.

Marilyn shook her head. Wishful thinking didn't make something true. And she'd already made a vow to herself before Jarryd had arrived that she wouldn't succumb to his charms unless he wanted the same thing she did—an exclusive, ongoing relationship. Unfortunately, a casual, no-commitment fling with him would only make things much harder for her in the long run, so that was off the table.

"I'm back," she called out.

Jarryd glanced up and smiled widely. "Ready to go?"

"Yes, as soon as I finish putting the flowers in a vase." She walked to a side table against the wall near the lounge and took the crystal vase displayed there. It was her favourite, and nothing else would do for the surprise gift Jarryd had given her.

Gah, she'd gone sentimental now, had she? How foolish.

She turned to head back to the kitchen counter where she'd left the bouquet and was surprised to see Jarryd there, starting to undo the wrapping from around the flower stems. "What are you doing?"

"I want to help you put these in that vase. Ruby gave me a mini-tutorial."

She chuckled at the picture of Lucas's florist mother teaching Jarryd how to arrange flowers. "What brought that on?"

"I bought a bunch from Ruby for my mum's birthday last month. I mentioned to her that when I took the flowers out of their binding and put them in a vase, they didn't look as good as when they came out of her shop, especially since the container I used had a wide mouth. So she taught me how to rearrange them."

"I see," she said with a grin. "I should let you do it, then."

"Yes, let me show you," Jarryd said with put-on superiority. He put water in the vase and plonked the flowers in it. Then he moved some stems here and there until he achieved the look he wanted. "Ta-dah!"

She clapped, laughing. "Ruby will be proud of you."

"The important question is," Jarryd said, stepping close to her and taking her by surprise with his sudden seriousness, "do you like them?"

She swallowed, his nearness robbing her lungs of oxygen. "Yes." Oh, God, that sounded too high-pitched. "Yes, I love them. Thank you," she said in a more normal tone, albeit breathless.

"Good," Jarryd mouthed, staring in her eyes.

And she stared right back, finding herself unwilling to break the connection... and wanting so much to kiss him.

Don't you dare, Marilyn Grant!

She stepped back and trained her gaze to the flowers. "Let's go to dinner so you can tell me what you want to tell me," she said hurriedly.

Jarryd inhaled deeply. "Yes. We should."

*****

Marilyn laughed out loud at Jarryd's description of a funny Christmas party invitation he'd recently received. She should be surprised that she could feel so relaxed with him as he drove them to the restaurant, but she really wasn't. She'd always known that she and Jarryd had a great rapport. Clearly, that hadn't disappeared.

And their physical chemistry hadn't gone anywhere, either—at least, for her part. Her traitorous body was already seeking some bedroom action just by being with him in the enclosed space of his car. Even as she kept up with their conversation, she couldn't help but play in her mind how hot sex had been with him. Argh! She wanted her brain to be the one making the decisions tonight, not her body or heart.

"Here we are," Jarryd said, turning into the parking area of the Banjo Patterson Cottage Restaurant.

She hid a rueful smile. She loved this establishment, having been here a few times in the past. The old-world charm of the centuries-old sandstone building which housed the restaurant made everything feel more romantic. But if Jarryd disappointed her tonight by propositioning her for casual sex, it might just forever spoil this place for her.

Jarryd opened her car door and held out his hand. She took it as she got out of the car, but let go as they started to walk to the restaurant. All she needed to do was hold on to her self-control until this dinner was over. By then, she would know his real agenda and she could decide her next steps accordingly.

"Miss Grant!" the maître d' exclaimed. "I didn't know you were coming tonight."

"Hi, Hector," Marilyn said with a smile. "Jarryd here made the reservations tonight."

"Of course, sir," Hector said, acknowledging Jarryd before leading them to a table in a private room with views of the Parramatta River. The affable man informed them of the specials and took their drink orders.

"You come here a lot, obviously," Jarryd commented once Hector had left.

"This place is one of my parents' favourites. I've been here with them a few times before."

"I bet the table they originally reserved for me wasn't this private," Jarryd said with a grin. "This is great."

She smiled her relief. It had worried her that Jarryd might have been put out when Hector treated them like VIPs because of her. But she should have known that small things like that didn't bother Jarryd. He was an easy-going guy.

"You can tell me all you want to say to your heart's content," she teased. "Nothing stopping you now."

Jarryd exhaled heavily. "Okay."

Ah, he was nervous. Which increased her nerves too.

"So earlier today, I told you that I didn't mean what I said when I broke up with you," Jarryd said. "I had personal problems that I didn't quite know how to handle, and I guess I thought breaking up with you was better than getting you involved in them."

Her heart pounded in her chest. Jarryd was looking at her pleadingly, like he was willing her to say she understood. She nodded to keep him talking.

Jarryd leaned forward and stared into her eyes. "Some of the issues I've been grappling with are still ongoing. But there's one thing that I'm sure of despite everything that's still muddling me."

She gawked at the intensity in his gaze, her breathing shallowing.

"I miss you," Jarryd said softly, his stare unwavering.

Her chest heaved and she blinked repeatedly. He missed her. Her heart started dancing in her chest.

A server appeared, but Jarryd kept his eyes glued to her as he sat back in his seat to allow the man to set their drinks on the table.

And she couldn't look away from him either.

"May I take your order?" the server said.

"I'll have your fish special," she murmured, not even remembering what the dish was.

"I'll have the same," Jarryd said as he held her gaze.

"Certainly," the server responded, hastening away to give them back the privacy they clearly wanted.

"I miss you," Jarryd said again, his voice more insistent.

She wanted to respond in kind, but instead she asked, "What does that mean?"

"I'd love for us to start seeing each other again."

Her heart skipped before racing. "Why?"

"Because I miss you." The worry was clear on Jarryd's face.

"What I want to know is," she said, closing her eyes for a moment to stop her heart from overpowering her head, "what exactly do you miss?"

"You. The whole you."

"Not just the sex?" she asked, watching his face intently.

Jarryd's lips quirked upwards. "No, definitely not just the sex, even though I miss that a hell of a lot."

Marilyn suppressed her smile because she wasn't done interrogating him about his motives. But she couldn't help but feel happy. He missed *her*, and not just the sex.

"I'm not after a casual relationship, Jarryd," she said sternly, just so he truly understood where she was coming from.

"I'm not either," he said softly. "Not with you."

She gawked at him, wanting so much to believe he meant those words. He looked utterly sincere, but could she really give in so easily?

"I am so sorry for being such an idiot two months ago," Jarryd said, his tone earnest. "But my decision back then didn't have anything to do with how I feel for you even if I did say the stupidest things. I have no excuse apart from being totally out of my depth with the situation I found myself in. But I'm very clear about things now. I want to be back with you."

She filled her lungs slowly, her mind whirling with reasons why she shouldn't be so quick to take him back. But her heart was forcing her to think of the other side of the equation. Jarryd didn't have to come back to her. He could have easily found himself another woman to date. Heaven knew there were plenty who'd jump at the chance to be with this total hunk. Yet here he was, pleading with her. Didn't he deserve another chance? Didn't *they*?

"I want to be with you, Marilyn. I want so much to make us work. I *miss* you."

This time she didn't try to hide her happy smile.

Relief flashed on Jarryd's face. "God, I so want to kiss you," he murmured.

"I'm not done asking you questions."

He put on a chastened expression. "Fire away."

"Would you share with me the problems that got you muddled?"

Jarryd's brows furrowed. "Can I tell you about them when I'm ready, please? I will tell you eventually, just not now."

She frowned back at him. "I understand that there are things you want to keep to yourself. But if we're going to be dating again, I'd want to be able to help you through your issues. How can I do that if you won't give me an idea what they're about? I'd continue to worry, especially when it sounds like they're something major. Besides, wouldn't our relationship be *mainly* about sex if we're not sharing our problems with each other and being each other's comfort and support?"

"Give me your hands." Jarryd placed his on the table, palm open, so she could reach for them.

She did and Jarryd's fingers closed around hers.

"Aren't there things that some couples keep from each other?" he asked. "I mean, do your parents tell each other *everything*? I know mine don't. My dad keeps certain things from my mum if he knows she'll only get worried. I do intend to share most things with you, but just not these particular ones that cropped up two months ago. And like I said earlier, you'll still get to know about them eventually. Just not yet."

Marilyn stared at their interlocked fingers. She couldn't believe they were having this conversation. She hadn't meant to throw serious-relationship questions at him, but she'd felt comfortable enough—safe enough—to ask them. Didn't that show how close a connection she and Jarryd truly had?

She was happy to take things slow, as long as she and Jarryd had the same intention: a committed relationship that might end up being long-term, if that was where this journey took them.

"Okay," she said.

"Okay, what?"

"Okay to you missing me."

"And?"

"Okay to dating again."

Jarryd's face broke into a happy smile. "And okay to kissing you right now?"

Her answer was an inviting grin.

Jarryd swiftly got out of his chair, went to her, tilted her chin, then bent down to kiss her. Hungrily.

Marilyn cupped his face and kissed him back.

She waited for Jarryd to break the kiss, but he went on... and on. Finally, he stood back up, and she noticed Hector standing by the threshold.

With her parents next to him.

CHAPTER FIVE

Jarryd pulled back. He wanted to keep on kissing Marilyn, but he was getting too hot for her. And this wasn't the time and place to get a hard-on. He noticed her eyes rounding as she stared at something behind him.

He twisted to see what she was looking at and gulped involuntarily. Alice Grant smiled at him, although her surprise was still clear on her face. But Barry Grant, who looked as distinguished as he did in magazine photos, had a big scowl on his face.

Damn. This wasn't the way he'd wanted Marilyn's father to meet him.

"Hi, Mum, Dad," Marilyn said, "I didn't realise you'd be here tonight."

"It was a last-minute decision," Alice said, walking inside. "And Hector mentioned you're here."

"We'd like to join your table, if you don't mind." Barry's tone demanded agreement.

Marilyn's gaze flickered to Jarryd.

"Of course not, Mr. Grant," he answered with a smile, gesturing for a handshake. "I'm Jarryd Westbourne. Pleased to meet you."

"Hello," Barry replied, gripping his hand tightly. "Alice was just telling me about you on our way here."

Jarryd kept the grin plastered on his face, not having an instant response to that. Whatever good things Marilyn's mother had said about him might have been negated by what they'd just witnessed. He wouldn't be surprised if the Grants hated attracting attention in a public place, and there he'd been, devouring their daughter's mouth in one of their favourite restaurants. What timing.

A server arranged two extra places on their table, giving him time to get back his bearings—and swallow his disappointment. No more heart-to-heart talk or sweet kisses with Marilyn tonight in this place.

Time crawled for Jarryd as he fielded question after question from Barry. If it hadn't been for Marilyn and Alice interjecting with some light-hearted comments every so often, this dinner would simply have been an inquisition. In a way, he didn't mind. It wasn't everyday he got someone of Barry Grant's calibre talking business matters with him.

"What do you do to get new business?" Barry asked next.

"Currently, I'm lucky enough to have a steady stream coming from my list of contacts from my previous company, and also from referrals from my current clients. But I'm about to work with a marketing consultant to help me with branding and to also help me tap into the cold market."

"Can't rest on your laurels," Barry said, nodding. "And how's cash flow for you? From what you've said, you would have had to put in extra capital to feed your growth. Monthly obligations like interest repayments and wages could kill your momentum if your cash inflow is dry for a period of time."

"I do have to watch it carefully," he said simply.

Things were a lot better now after he'd decided to use the five million dollars Margaret had deposited in Westbourne Constructions' account without his consent a month before she passed away. He hadn't wanted to touch it at first, but Margaret had said to consider it as her investment in his company. Accepting that gift, which was separate from his inheritance, seemed to be the only way he could thank her for the love she'd shown him in the one year they'd gotten to know each other.

Marilyn started talking about the charity events she'd been organising for the Christmas season. To Jarryd's relief, Barry had stopped giving him the third degree to discuss Marilyn's plans.

Phew.

*****

"Please let me get this," Jarryd said, pulling out his credit card from his wallet and holding it up for Hector to take.

"No," Barry said definitively, handing his black Amex to Hector, who grabbed it without hesitation.

Jarryd suppressed his sigh. At the very least, he wanted to pay for his and Marilyn's dinner considering this had turned out to be their reconciliation date. But now wasn't the time to get into a competition with Barry over who was the boss.

"How about we give you a lift home, Marilyn?" Barry said. "Your place is out of Jarryd's way. It's easier for us."

"I don't mind driving her home, sir," he said quickly.

"It's late," Barry said with a dismissive gesture. "Saves you from going over the bridge only to come back again."

Jarryd glanced at Marilyn, who was frowning at her dad. She wasn't happy either, but she was staying quiet.

He felt like saying that he and Marilyn were mature adults who didn't need their parents chauffeuring them around, but he decided to follow Marilyn's lead and not argue further.

Was Barry trying to ensure that Jarryd didn't get any more time with Marilyn tonight? Jarryd hoped he was mistaken in his assumption that Barry didn't like him. It wasn't anything Marilyn's dad had said, but a vibe the man had been exuding.

Barry finished paying for their dinner and they all walked out of the restaurant. The Grants' Bentley was hard to miss, parked in a spot marked *Authorised Vehicles Only*. They stopped beside it.

"Well, it was a lovely dinner, wasn't it?" Alice said.

"It was," Jarryd answered. "Thank you both for the meal, and for joining us."

"You're welcome, Jarryd. We hope to see you again soon." Alice kissed him goodbye.

Barry shook his hand, but the man had an inscrutable expression. He really couldn't tell what Barry Grant thought of him.

"I'll just walk Jarryd to his car," Marilyn said to her parents.

"Okay, darling," Alice said, whispering something to her daughter before getting inside their vehicle.

"Do you think your dad likes me?" Jarryd asked Marilyn in a low voice as they strolled a few metres to where they'd parked earlier.

"Yes," Marilyn said. "Otherwise he would have given you the silent treatment. In fact, I'd say he was impressed with the way you answered all of his questions tonight."

"Really? But why doesn't he want me to take you home?"

"Dad's kind of… overprotective," Marilyn said with hesitation. "That's why I'm going home with them, so I can tell him what he wants to know about you. That'll stop him from…"

He glanced at her. Marilyn was clearly embarrassed. "From what?"

"Googling you or asking other people about you."

"Really? He'll do that?"

Marilyn sighed, facing him as they reached his car. "Three years ago, I dated a guy who got a managerial job at one of Grant Ace's competitors. Dad plays golf with someone who used to be a board member there and he informed Dad that my then-boyfriend had relayed sensitive information about Grant Ace to his bosses. Turned out that the bastard I was going out with had overheard my parents and me talking about this deal. Grant Ace lost out because of what that loser did."

"You're kidding," he said in disbelief.

"Dad was apoplectic and I felt extremely betrayed. After that, I kind of stopped dating seriously. That was why Mum was happy to meet you—because she hated that I'd let that one event affect me so much. As for Dad…

well, I just need to convince him what a nice, trustworthy guy you are," she said with a smile.

Jarryd caressed Marilyn's cheek. How he wanted to punch the fucker who'd dared hurt her like that!

And he also forcefully pushed away the guilt that pinched him.

He wasn't like Marilyn's ex. He had no intention whatsoever of betraying her trust. He just needed to keep a few things from her for the time being—things that had nothing to do with her, her parents or their companies. No need for him to feel guilty, right?

"Hey, I'm okay now," Marilyn said, circling her arms around his neck. "That was three years ago."

He smiled and placed his hands on her waist. He would have pulled her flush against him, but he bet her parents were watching. God, he wanted so badly to spend the night with her. "Can I see you tomorrow?"

She shook her head. "I have meetings tomorrow for some charity work. How about Tuesday or Wednesday night? I'm free then."

"Yes, but I can only meet you for short lunches during the weekdays. I have a project that's running well behind schedule and my staff and I will be working overtime all week. What about next Saturday?"

"I'll be at Mum and Dad's for dinner then. They want to discuss business. Actually, Mum wants me to take you along," Marilyn said with a laugh. "As if you'd want to spend more time with them so soon after Dad's incessant questioning tonight."

Jarryd shrugged. "He couldn't have many more questions to ask, could he? Especially after you fill him in on your way home?"

Marilyn cocked her head. "Are you saying you want to go with me to my parents' for dinner on Saturday?"

He stared at Marilyn. They seemed to be careering again like they did before, like they had no idea how to take things slow. But did he really care? If they hadn't broken up two months ago, they probably would be in this exact situation right now anyway—him meeting her parents. "Would your dad mind if I do go?"

"I don't think so, especially since he'll have that time to grill you even more. He'll definitely think we're serious."

"Would you mind if they think we're serious?"

"We're going very fast, aren't we?" she murmured.

"I know, but I can't help it. I don't want to scare you off, though, so I'll back off a bit if you want me to."

A smile played on Marilyn's face, then she shook her head. "I'm happy to go with the flow if you are."

His chest expanded. "Can I kiss you right now? With your parents watching?"

Marilyn laughed and pulled his head down to hers for a quick kiss on the lips. "Why don't you come to my place for lunch on Saturday?" she murmured. "We can spend all afternoon together before going to my parents' for dinner."

"Great idea." He gave her another peck, then watched her walk back to her parents' car. He couldn't wait for next Saturday to come.

*****

Jarryd's breath left him when Marilyn opened her door. She was wearing a pair of very short denim shorts and a nude-coloured tank top—sans bra. He banged the door shut, pulled her against him and went straight for her mouth.

Marilyn giggled. "Hello to you too."

"We have lots of catching up to do," he said, running his hands down her back and resting them on her tush. "Those one-hour lunches and late-night phone calls were nowhere near enough. I couldn't touch you like this then."

"I'm right in the middle of preparing our lunch," Marilyn said breathlessly.

"We don't need food. We have each other."

Marilyn laughed out loud as she untangled herself from him and led him towards the kitchen. "We need energy for what you have in mind."

"What are we having?"

"Hamburgers and salad." Marilyn went to the kitchen counter and tossed the ingredients that were in a big bowl. "Just about finished with this, then I'll grill the burgers."

He snaked his arms around her waist and nuzzled her cheek. "Have I told you I haven't had much sleep at all this past week? Kept thinking of you."

"Yes, you've told me," she said with a smile in her voice.

"I couldn't stop thinking about what would have happened if your parents hadn't crashed our date last week."

"You haven't told me *exactly* what you thought might have happened if they hadn't turned up at the restaurant."

He sucked in a breath. His cock had already been hard in the car on his way here from all the images that kept playing in his head. He pressed himself against her back so she could feel his hard-on.

Marilyn inhaled sharply and stopped what she was doing. Then she turned around and curved her arms around his neck.

Jarryd grinned, pinning her against the benchtop with his body. "If they hadn't arrived, we would have played footsie while finishing our dinner," he said, grinding his crotch against hers.

Marilyn half-gasped and half-chuckled.

"We wouldn't have had dessert, because we would have been in a hurry to get home. In fact, we would have started making out in the car."

"Really?" Marilyn asked, rubbing her leg against his.

"Oh, yeah. And I wouldn't have been able to help doing this while I kissed you." He thumbed her nipple while he plunged his tongue into her sweet mouth.

Marilyn raked her fingers through his hair, kissing him back with equal fervour.

"And," he grunted breathlessly after a long moment, "we would have sped home before we totally lost all control in the car park."

"And once we got here, we would have stumbled out of the car and walked through that door," Marilyn said against his lips, pointing to the exit to her garage.

"Uh-huh." He didn't bother telling her that since they'd driven his car last night, they would have had to enter via her front door. No way he'd spoil their game with trivial facts when Marilyn was enjoying it as much as he was.

"Then we would have ended up right here," Marilyn continued, undoing his fly. "And we would have stripped each other's clothes off."

"Ah, well, that's not the next step I'd imagined," he said, hiding his grin by kissing her shoulder.

"It wasn't?"

"No. See, what I would have done next was this." He lifted her and sat her on a clean spot on her long countertop. Then, staring at her heatedly, he spread her legs and stood in between them.

"Oh. And then what?" Marilyn asked, her breathing shallow.

He took her tank top off her.

"And?" she mouthed.

He started with her lips, kissing them softly yet insistently before travelling to her neck and throat. Then he left a trail of soft kisses down her chest, enjoying the feel of her heated skin with his lips. Her nipples were already hard and he licked one of them, rolling his tongue around it.

"Jarryd," Marilyn whispered, arching her back to him.

"I imagined savouring every part of your body first," he murmured, closing his mouth on the other pebbled peak and suckling.

Marilyn wrapped both her legs around his waist, pulling her to him as she inched her bottom closer to the edge of the counter. Her mound nestled against his erection, making him groan out loud. Now, this was better than he'd imagined. But he wasn't ready to lose control yet.

"These are sexy," he said, undoing the button of her shorts. "But they're sexier on the floor."

"Yes, take them off," Marilyn said impatiently, lifting her bum so he could pull her clothing down her legs.

"Can't wait, baby?" He ran teasing fingers along her inner thigh.

Marilyn grabbed his shirt to pull him close. "Of course I can," she breathed, kissing him passionately while her groin sought contact with the bulge in his pants. "I'm just thinking of you. I don't want you to have blue balls."

He chuckled. "Aw, how sweet of you, honey. There I was thinking you'd like me to pay attention to this first." He put his hand between their bodies and groaned when he reached her soaked entrance. He wet his finger with her juices before using it to rub her clit.

Marilyn moaned, throwing her head back.

His dick jerked. There was nothing like his Marilyn looking so damned hot and horny to heighten his arousal. Eager to please her further, he bent down and replaced his fingers with his tongue. Ah, he loved pleasuring her like this, loved tasting the part of her that would give him sheer ecstasy very soon.

He felt Marilyn's hand caressing his head. He looked up and found her looking at him with half-closed eyes, breathing through her mouth.

"I missed you," she said, giving him a sweet, lustful smile.

That did it. He needed to be inside her. Now.

CHAPTER SIX

Marilyn felt bereft when Jarryd abruptly stood up and got out of his clothes.

Biting back a smile, she jumped down from the counter. She was more than ready for him, but she wanted to drive him a little crazier like he'd done to her.

"Hey, get back up there," Jarryd said, pulling out a condom from the pocket of his denims.

"You can't have all the fun." She grasped his erection as she kissed his neck.

Jarryd inhaled sharply.

Staring into his eyes, she caressed his lips with a finger before she kissed and licked her way down his muscular torso. Oh, how she'd missed this body. Unable to wait any longer, she kneeled and ran her tongue slowly along his engorged length.

"Babe," Jarryd said in a gasp, which became a grunt when she put him in her mouth. "I love this, but I'm dying to be inside you, sweetheart."

She smiled, ignoring his half-hearted protest. A few more sucks and tugs should have him begging—

"Baby, now, please," Jarryd said.

"Please, what?" she asked with a grin.

Jarryd hauled her up onto the counter and hurriedly put on the condom. Then he was back standing between her parted legs.

"This," he said, stroking her nub with the head of his erection before pushing into her waiting core.

"Ahh," she gasped, leaning back and propping up her body with her elbows. Oh, he was hitting that spot inside which focused her attention solely on the pleasure evoked by his hardness going in and out of her. It was just as good as she remembered. No one had ever aroused her or given her pleasure like Jarryd could.

Moans bubbled out of her throat, unbidden.

"So good. So fucking good," Jarryd mumbled through gritted teeth, his breathing laboured. "You have no idea how much I missed this."

"Yes... more..." Marilyn said mindlessly, tightening her legs around him.

Jarryd hissed, driving into her faster. "You want this too?" He placed his thumb on her clit and rubbed in circles while he tirelessly thrust into her over and over.

She keened, lost to everything but the sensations Jarryd was expertly stimulating. When Jarryd leaned down to suck on her nipple also, she cried out, her body convulsing in an intense orgasm that went on and on.

"Fuck... yes... keep squeezing me..." Jarryd said almost incoherently. His hips pumped harder. Faster. Out of control. Triggering another orgasm that had her gasping for air.

Then Jarryd yelled as he erupted inside her. Loud and long.

It took a few moments before she was able to move and throw her arms around Jarryd's neck. She rested herself on his frame, feeling like the usual blissful boneless mass she often became after they made love.

"That was incredible," Jarryd said against her hair, holding her tight.

"And you wonder why I never believed you when you said we had no spark," she quipped.

Jarryd laughed. "What time do we need to be at your parents' tonight?"

"Six thirty."

"Good. Because I need to be shown again and again how wrong I was to have said those words. How about you teach me my lesson in your bedroom and the shower?"

She lifted her head from his shoulder to grin at him. "I need lunch first. I missed breakfast."

Jarryd kissed her nose. "Then let me grill those burgers right now so we can eat. Then I'm carrying you to your bedroom afterwards."

"Okay." She'd love to see Jarryd cook naked. That would definitely whet her appetite for more.

*****

Marilyn stretched in the passenger seat, feeling languid, as Jarryd parked his car outside her parents' house. She would have loved a nap after hours of passionate lovemaking, but she was also excited about taking Jarryd to her parents' home. He'd be the first date she'd taken there in three years.

"You're so beautiful," Jarryd said as he turned off the engine. "I love that look of sexual afterglow on you."

She gasped, sitting up straight. "I don't want to look like that in front of my parents."

Jarryd grinned. "I don't know if you can help it."

While she knew that Jarryd was only teasing, she still brought the sun visor down to check herself on its small mirror. Considering that she'd climaxed a number of times in one afternoon, she wouldn't be surprised if she did have "sexual afterglow" painted all over her face.

"I'm sure they won't notice," Jarryd said with a chuckle as he got out of the car, then came around to open her door for her.

"Are you nervous about tonight? Being on Mum and Dad's turf?" she asked as she got out.

"Nah. As long as your dad doesn't point a shotgun at me for putting that I-had-multiple-orgasms-today look on your face, I'll be fine."

She pushed him away playfully, and Jarryd wrapped his arms around her, chuckling as he kissed her forehead. Then he retrieved the hazelnut mousse cake from the portable cooler in the boot of the car—bought from her dad's favourite patisserie.

Sighing in contentment, she took his hand as they made their way to the front door of her parents' Federation-style mansion.

Funny how she was so relaxed about this dinner. The last guy she'd brought here was that moron who'd betrayed her. But she trusted Jarryd. And she'd been impressed with him at the restaurant last week. He hadn't fawned over her folks and neither had he acted like someone with a chip on his shoulder who expected her parents to look down on him.

He'd been great. Absolutely wonderful. She wasn't even worried anymore that there were things he wasn't ready to share with her. At least he'd been upfront about having to keep certain things to himself.

Marilyn pressed the security intercom and her dad opened the door after a short wait.

"Hi, Dad," she said, kissing him on the cheek. She hid a smile, surprised at seeing him wearing a colourful apron dotted with different types of flowers. Her father was one of the hardest-working people she knew, but he would rather eat out or bring in a private chef than work in the kitchen. She wondered how her mother had succeeded in getting him to help cook tonight.

"Hello, darling," Barry said, hugging her before shaking hands with Jarryd.

"Thank you for having me here tonight, sir," Jarryd said.

"Pleasure," Barry said in a clipped tone, eyeing the box Jarryd was carrying.

"Yes, it's your favourite," Marilyn said, flashing him a please-be-nice-to-Jarryd smile.

Barry lifted an eyebrow at her.

"Marilyn told me that this dessert is the best way to butter you up, Mr. Grant," Jarryd said, holding up the box to Barry. "Since I really want you to like me, I thought I'd hand it to you myself. I'll even go so far as to offer you my slice if you promise not to kick me out of your house if I happen to hug your daughter in front of you tonight."

Barry's jaw dropped as he stared at Jarryd, his eyes round.

Marilyn held her breath, her own eyes bugged out as she watched the two men. Goodness, what had gotten into Jarryd?

"It's this apron, isn't it?" Barry finally said, wincing as he looked down at his attire.

Jarryd shrugged, grinning widely. "It does soften your aura, sir."

Barry sighed. "Tell you what. How about you tell my wife that Marilyn can help her in the kitchen while I give you a tour around the house, and I'll let you keep your slice of that cake."

Marilyn gasped. "Hey, not fair! I was looking forward to showing Jarryd around." She was tickled pink, though, that her father didn't get mad at Jarryd.

"Then how can I give him a piece of my mind without you listening?" Barry asked, deadpan.

Oh, no. "Dad, he was only joking."

"It's okay, honey," Jarryd said. "I'll take what I deserve. As long as he doesn't make me wear that apron."

Barry laughed out loud, shaking his head. "You've got spunk, Jarryd. I like that. Let's go to the kitchen, kids, or Alice will wonder if I've run Jarryd off."

Marilyn linked her arm with Jarryd's as they followed Barry to the back of the house. "I'm so impressed," she whispered to him.

"Good," Jarryd whispered back. "You can give me my reward later."

"Hello!" Alice called out as they appeared in the kitchen.

"Jarryd's helping you, love," Barry said, taking the box of dessert from Jarryd. "His only condition is that he doesn't wear any apron."

"Barry," Alice said with censure.

"Happy to help, Mrs. Grant," Jarryd said. "Mr. Grant has agreed that he won't give me the evil eye when I kiss Marilyn in front of him."

"Kiss?" Barry boomed. "You said you were only going to hug her."

"Well, we didn't talk about relieving you of your kitchen duties before, sir. Just making sure everything's fair."

Marilyn chuckled at the incredulous look on her mother's face at the exchange between the men. "Dad likes Jarryd. He thinks he's spunky," she said.

"Well, isn't it great that you're getting along like a house on fire," Alice said to the guys. "But you're not getting out of helping me here, Barry Grant. Jarryd is our guest and Marilyn will be entertaining him while we finish preparing dinner."

Barry let out a heavy breath. "Okay. But let me talk business with Marilyn first for about ten minutes."

"Anything to get you out of the kitchen, huh, Dad?" Marilyn teased.

"So we won't have to interrupt our night with business talk later," Barry said innocently.

"Okay," Alice conceded. "Don't be too long, you two. Jarryd, sit down, please. You're not lifting a finger on your first dinner with us."

Marilyn followed her father to his study, giving Jarryd a brief wave goodbye.

"Obviously, you and Jarryd are getting serious," Barry said as he closed the door. "You said you started dating three months ago?"

"Yes." She didn't see a reason to tell her dad that they had been on a break for a whole two months of that time.

"Aren't things going too fast?"

"I thought you wanted to talk business, Dad."

Barry faced her fully. "I've never seen you so taken by anyone before, Marilyn. I know you've asked me to ease up on Jarryd, but it's natural for me to worry. I don't want you getting swept up by your feelings before you get to know him well."

She smiled wryly. "I thought we were going too fast as well. But it feels right. And I trust Jarryd."

"It might *feel* right. It doesn't necessarily mean it *is* right. And what's your basis for fully trusting him?"

"Jarryd was my friend first before we went out together," she reasoned in a measured tone. "And you can ask Rick or Lucas or the Carmichael brothers about him. He's friends with them too. Besides, I've never felt more... comfortable or... at ease or... I can't explain it. I just feel that Jarryd and I are meant for each other." Oh God, what had made her blurt that sappy statement out?

But that was exactly how she felt.

"Has he told you he loves you?"

She blushed. "I think it's way too early for *that*."

"Good. It's good to wait. Be sure of his feelings for you first. What some people think is love might have more to do with being attracted to our wealth and social status than anything else."

She opened her mouth to defend Jarryd, but Barry held up a hand to halt her.

"I'm not saying that Jarryd is only using you or that he's only after your money. I actually like what I see

71

so far. He's not scared to offend me and that's saying a lot. All I'm advising you is get to know him better before you start thinking that he might be the one."

Too late. She was already believing that Jarryd was the one. But she nodded to appease her father. "Don't worry, Dad."

Barry stared at her for a moment, then smiled. "Your mother told you we want to make a bid for Well of Brilliance."

"Yes."

Barry took two files out from his drawer and dropped them on his desk. "Here's all the information about the company, and here's the proposal that we'll be putting up on Friday to Lorna and Ben Tramwell, the siblings who own it. They're not going to make a decision until after the new year, but they want to know that our offer is competitive enough so they can advise Greeves Minerals that there's another offer on the table that they want to consider. Apparently, they were close to finalising the deal until we contacted them. We'll have to prepare for a bidding war. Fortunately, we'll get to enjoy the holidays first before that happens."

"That gives me time to make my decision, then," she said.

"Marilyn, I can't see why you'd want to limit yourself to your business brokering firm. You've already proven to everyone that you'll be more than capable of heading a company like Well of Brilliance if we happen to be successful in acquiring it. And if we lose out on it, I still want you back at Grant Ace. What I'd do if I were you is to start letting your second-in-command sit at the helm. Free yourself to work with us again."

"You're not gonna stop bugging me until I say yes, right?" she asked dryly.

"Do you really not see yourself working for Grant Ace again? Do you just want your share of the profits without being actively involved in steering the company?"

"No," she admitted. "I've always known I'll go back to work there. It's a matter of when."

"I'd say this is the right time."

"Maybe. Let me go through those documents."

"If you're in, it's better that you're in from the beginning. So I suggest you make your decision before we submit the proposal, so you can make suggestions or changes to it before then."

She could see the sense in that. "Okay."

"Good! Now let's go rejoin your mum and your boyfriend."

She smiled, thrilled that it had been easy for her dad to refer to Jarryd as her boyfriend. "What help are you supposed to give Mum?" she asked as they left the study.

"She wants me to stir-fry the veggies while she grills the salmon. How about you do it for me?"

She smirked. "I'm giving Jarryd a tour of the house. But don't worry. You won't have to help clean up later."

"When did you grow up and stop obeying me?" he asked with faux authority.

"A long, long time ago, Daddy," she said with a chuckle, hugging him as they walked back into the kitchen.

Jarryd was sitting on a stool by the island bench, a glass of wine in his hand and a bowl of nuts in front of him while he chatted with her mother. Jarryd beamed when he spotted her.

Her heart skipped, excited to see him again. Gosh, she had it bad. But she wasn't complaining at all.

"Business talk finished?" Alice asked them as she pulled something from the fridge.

"For tonight," Barry said. "Oh, by the way, Marilyn. Have you decided if you want to appear on *Biz Q&A*? Aren't you supposed to answer Patrick soon?"

Jarryd's strangled coughing startled Marilyn.

"You okay?" she asked, hurrying to him. He wasn't choking on a nut, was he?

CHAPTER SEVEN

Jarryd nodded his thanks to Alice as he took the glass of water she'd hurriedly handed to him. He took large gulps, soothing the tickle that had lodged in his throat from his surprise at Barry's words.

Patrick O'Neill had invited *Marilyn* to appear on *Biz Q&A*?

Had Patrick found out that he was going out with Marilyn, and was this Patrick's way of telling him who had the upper hand?

"You okay?" Marilyn repeated, rubbing his back and looking at him with concern.

He hacked one last time to totally get rid of the discomfort. "The wine just went down the wrong way. I'm okay now."

"Thank goodness it wasn't a nut," Alice said. "Well, we should be ready to eat in about twenty minutes. How about you two do the house tour before then?"

"Okay," Marilyn said, raising her eyebrows questioningly at Jarryd.

He nodded eagerly, keen to be alone with her.

Marilyn took his hand and showed him the formal living areas first, sharing with him her fond memories of the place. He pushed aside his nagging worries to concentrate on Marilyn's stories and to admire the property, which really was something special. The period features had been kept and maintained, blending well with the modern, comfortable furnishings and impressive art collection.

They stepped out into the vast outdoor entertaining area, punctuated by the oval-shaped swimming pool, and went back inside again through a set of double doors leading to the library with floor-to-ceiling shelving filled with books. It was hard not to be impressed with the house's understated grandeur and the homey feel that permeated it.

Marilyn quickly showed him the study, powder room and a downstairs guest room before they headed upstairs, where Marilyn started with the two spacious guest rooms. Then she showed him her parents' impressive master suite, with its own sitting room, study, cavernous dressing room and stunning bathroom with marble floors.

"There used to be six big bedrooms up here when my parents bought the house when I was around ten," Marilyn said. "Then when Mum and Dad had it renovated, they took three of the bedrooms to form this suite into the sanctuary they'd always wanted."

"It's a beautiful house. Very solid bones and full of character and warmth," he said, admiring the detailing on the cornices.

"Yeah. I even stayed until I was twenty-one before I moved out, when my parents bought me my current place. In the beginning, I felt like coming back here was coming home. But working on the renovations at my place for two long years finally made me feel like my house *is* my home."

Jarryd looked at her in surprise. "It took two years to renovate your place?"

"Because I wanted the salary I earned to pay for the renovations, not the money that came from the family trust fund. So I had my place done up little by little, as I was able to afford it."

He smiled at her, more than impressed. Marilyn could have grown up a spoiled brat, being an only daughter of ultra-wealthy parents who were quite obviously supportive. But she hadn't.

"What?" Marilyn asked with a laugh as he continued to stare.

He pulled her to him. "You're so special," he murmured.

She snickered. "Why? Because I used money that was a product of my hard work to pay for my home renovations? I don't think that makes me special. You'll find millions of others doing that around the world. Heck, I didn't even buy my own house, so you could say I'm less than impressive."

"You know what I mean."

She shrugged. "I've learnt long ago that being wealthy has its own set of drawbacks. Sometimes they can be extreme. There are people who never bother to get to know me, and only see me for who my parents are, not for who I am. Either they put me down, believing I'm just another rich bitch who'd thumb my nose at them, or they put me on a pedestal, thinking knowing me is the best thing for their careers, social life, or whatnot. I'm not saying that to complain, because I know how blessed I am—how lucky. All I'm saying is as far as I'm concerned, whoever we are, we all have challenges and blessings—

just in varied areas of our lives. Some people have big issues with money, but they're lucky in love. Some have health problems, but they're rich with support from friends and family. Others are estranged from their loved ones, but are setting the world on fire with their careers. What I'm trying to say is we all hurt and rejoice, just for different reasons. In that sense, we're really all equals."

Jarryd gawked at her, touched by her words.

He was trying to tell her she was special *to him*. But was this her way of saying she didn't care that he was a guy of average means while she came from a rich family? That she saw him as nothing less than her equal?

That was so sweet, but he didn't want to discuss financial status right now. The time wasn't right. He'd have to outright lie if they did. "You haven't shown me your old bedroom yet," he said to change the subject.

Marilyn grinned. "This way."

He followed her to the room at the far end of the hallway. Marilyn opened the door and he was greeted with furnishings similar to the ones she had at her place—which instantly reminded him of what they'd done in her bed before they'd come here. "How many times do you stay here overnight?"

"Not very often. Usually only when we have parties here and I don't feel like driving home after having too much to drink." Marilyn ran her hand on the bedspread in a smoothing gesture.

Jarryd's cock stirred. Marilyn and her bed. He knew what he'd prefer to do with both right here, right now, but it wasn't possible. Still, he couldn't help but tease at the very least. "Would be nice for us to try that bed," he murmured, looking at her lasciviously.

Marilyn's eyes widened. "Now?"

"I didn't have a particular time in mind, but since you've said the word *now*…" He pulled her flush against him.

Marilyn gasped. "Dinner is almost ready. They'd look for us if we're gone for longer than expected."

"We still have about,"—he checked his watch—"six minutes. That's enough for a quickie."

"You can't be serious."

Biting back his laughter, he kissed her passionately.

He'd expected her to resist, but Marilyn let out a soft moan, curving her arms around his neck and moulding her body to his.

His dick got hard with the speed that only Marilyn could arouse. "I'm only joking, honey," he murmured against her lips. "I don't want your parents to have a bad impression of me."

"Don't tell me you're choosing my parents over me," Marilyn said, her oh-so-naughty hand going to his crotch and rubbing.

"Babe," he groaned, stopping her as his erection got bigger. "Don't, please. I can't have a hard-on right now."

"I can't believe you just said that."

"You're such a tease."

"You started it."

He gave her a loud kiss before moving away from her. "Let's get out of here or I won't get the image of you naked and writhing under me out of my head."

"Ugh, now who's being a tease?" Marilyn said with a glare before heading out of the room.

He grinned. "Good to know I'm not the only one feeling frustrated here."

Marilyn chuckled.

He adjusted himself as he followed her, his dick still uncomfortably hard. He better think of something that would make it go down before they rejoined Alice and Barry.

What about the reason for his coughing fit earlier? His erection softened quickly. He couldn't believe he'd almost forgotten about that. "Hey, what's with you being invited to *Biz Q&A*?" he asked nonchalantly.

"Oh, that. Well, Patrick O'Neill originally wanted Dad or Mum to appear on the show as a mentor, but they both declined," Marilyn said as they climbed down the stairs. "Then Patrick called me. It seems he's keen for one of us Grants to be on the show. I'm finding it hard to make up my mind, though. I'm still tossing over the pros and cons of it in my head."

"I guess the biggest thing would be the loss of some of the privacy you enjoy now."

"Yeah, that's the main drawback that I can think of. But my parents are thinking of acquiring another business that they want me to head, so appearing on *Biz Q&A* might actually be a good move if I decide to return to the Grant Ace fold."

His heart thudded hard. No way he'd want Marilyn to work with Patrick O'Neill. "What business are your parents planning to buy?"

"A company that retails gemstones. It's all hush-hush at this point, so I can't talk about it, but my parents want me to tell them if I'm in or not by Friday."

He swallowed hard. A company that retailed gemstones? Not Well of Brilliance, surely.

"Great timing," Barry said as they walked into the kitchen. "Dinner's just about ready."

Jarryd did his utmost to push his worries aside during dinner, but it was difficult. Fortunately, most of the conversation centred around Marilyn's childhood in the mansion, and Alice was more than happy to do most of the talking.

Soon, dinner was over, to his relief.

"Jarryd and I will do the cleaning up," Marilyn said during a lull in the conversation after they'd finished dessert.

Alice and Barry happily stepped out to the pool area to enjoy the rest of their wine outside.

"Is everything okay?" Marilyn asked when they were alone.

"Yeah. Why?"

"Just sensed that you were somewhere else at times while we were eating."

"Yeah, I was still upstairs in your old bedroom," he said in a loud whisper.

"Oh, really? But you didn't look like you were thinking about sex."

He suppressed a sigh. "Actually, the mention of *Biz Q&A* earlier reminded me of a problem at work that I'll have to deal with first thing Monday morning."

"Something stressful?" Marilyn asked sympathetically as she transferred some leftovers to a smaller dish.

"A bit. You know how it is with delayed projects."

"You want to call it a night after we finish here so you can have a good rest? We did have a very tiring afternoon," she said with a grin.

He chuckled, warmth suffusing him both from her sweetness and her naughtiness. "You know, I think I'll need more loving than rest tonight for me to feel completely relaxed for Monday."

"Uh-huh. Who are you gonna call for that?" Marilyn asked as she started to load the dishwasher.

"What?"

"I said who are you gonna call for that?"

Did Marilyn not hear him right? "I said I'll need more *loving* tonight."

Marilyn glanced up at him, her expression casual. "Yeah, I heard you."

"*Who am I gonna call for some sex?*" he asked incredulously.

"Yes," she said, deadpan.

He scowled at her, his chest compressing. Hadn't they agreed this *wasn't* a casual relationship?

A goofy grin appeared on Marilyn's face. "So I'm the only one you want, right?"

"What do you think?" he asked with a huff.

Marilyn walked to him, a cute, irresistible, forgive-me smile on her beautiful face. "Just teasing you."

"If your parents weren't close by, I'd give you a smack on that hot bum of yours for asking such a ridiculous question," he said with a growl.

Marilyn giggled. "I think it's the wine. It's making me playful."

And just like that, she'd made him horny again.

"Can we go home after cleaning up here?" Jarryd asked in a low voice, sending her a heated look. He would have taken her in his arms, but that would guarantee an obvious erection that he couldn't afford with her parents about.

"Okay," Marilyn said readily, running a hand down his chest. "Then I can give you all the loving you need."

He inhaled through his mouth. "Chop-chop, then. Let's finish up here quick smart."

They did finish cleaning up in record time.

And Marilyn did give him incredible loving that went on for the whole weekend.

He hated that he had to lie to her about why he had to leave her bed so early on Monday morning. But he had a meeting with the CEO and COO of Greeves Minerals.

CHAPTER EIGHT

Jarryd walked down the corridor leading to several meeting rooms in the Greeves Minerals headquarters in Sydney. He wasn't looking forward to this meeting with Olivia Greeves and her son Elliot—who was now the company's chief operating officer. Olivia and Elliot each owned twenty-five percent of Greeves Minerals, since they'd received the shares that would have gone to Harold and Margaret's son when Harold had died.

Lilah, the young receptionist, let him inside a modern light-filled room with a round six-seater table in the middle. "Mrs. Greeves and Mr. Greeves will be with you shortly, Mr. Westbourne. Can I get you anything in the meantime?"

"I'm fine, thank you, Lilah."

The receptionist closed the door and Jarryd looked around, that surreal feeling descending on him again. It was plain crazy. He had little knowledge about mining or the workings of this multibillion dollar company, yet his slice of the pie was larger than anybody else's. Whatever did he plan to do with it? What the hell was he doing here?

"Hello, Jarryd."

He twisted to smile at Olivia Greeves, who looked striking in her black suit and white dress shirt. He gestured for a handshake. "Olivia, good to see you again."

"Thank you. You too. Elliot is still on a phone call, but he won't be long. Have a seat, please."

"Thank you." Jarryd sat on the leather chair opposite Olivia.

"Have you decided whether or not to sell us some or all of your shares?" Olivia asked.

He hid a smirk. Olivia was straight to the point. "Not yet. I'd really like to take my time before I make a decision. Right now I'm happy with the current arrangement—to be a shareholder and leave the management of the company to you guys."

Olivia nodded. If she was disappointed by his answer, she didn't let on.

Part of him did want to sell his stake in the company to Olivia and Elliot as soon as possible. After all, they were the ones running the show. Mother and son had worked here for years in managerial positions under Harold and Margaret's direction, and this business had to mean more to them than it did to him.

But Margaret had chosen to leave *him* her fifty-percent shareholding in Greeves Minerals. That fact had a massive effect on his decision. Even though his adoptive parents were loving and wonderful folks, Margaret O'Neill had plugged a hole in his heart that he hadn't even realised existed until they'd met. He was still grieving for his birth mother, who'd shown him genuine love in the one year they'd known each other, so he couldn't bear to sell the shares. It touched him deeply that he'd meant that much to Margaret.

Plus, he had that secondary reason of not wanting to touch his inheritance while Patrick was thinking of challenging the will. He didn't want anyone questioning his honesty.

The door opened and in came Elliot—a slightly built man who was about his age. "Sorry I'm late," Elliot said, extending his hand towards Jarryd.

Jarryd stood up and shook it. "No problem. I just got here myself."

"So have you decided to sell us your shares?" Elliot asked as he sat down.

"I was just telling Olivia that I'm happy with the status quo for the time being."

Elliot stared at him, clearly dismayed. "What makes you want to hold on to the shares? Were you always interested in mining companies?"

Jarryd gave him a tight smile. "It's a good investment, from what I've learnt about the company so far. Plus, Margaret did leave me the shares. I want to make the right decision regarding them."

Elliot sat back in his chair, arms locked behind his neck. "Did she really leave them to you?"

"Elliot," Olivia said sharply.

Jarryd narrowed his eyes. "What do you mean, Elliot?"

"You have to admit it's highly suspicious that Aunt Margaret would leave you almost all of her wealth when she'd only known you for a year."

"She did give birth to him, Elliot," Olivia said, her tone warning her son to back off.

Elliot smirked. "I'm just saying."

"I expect that my decision to keep the shares will not affect the way you run the company," Jarryd said, holding his temper even though angry heat rose up to his face.

"Of course not," Olivia answered placatingly. "We care about this company."

"Yes, *we* do," Elliot said.

"Good," he said with icy calm. "Now, is there anything else we need to talk about?"

"Nope," Elliot said. "Pity you had to come all the way here. You could have told us your decision over the phone."

"I thought I'd let you know face-to-face, just to be polite."

"Look, Jarryd, I apologise for Elliot's outburst," Olivia interjected. "We're just still surprised—shocked, actually—about you and Margaret's will. We never knew you existed until after her death."

Jarryd took a deep breath. Hell, even he was still incredulous about the whole thing. And even though he resented having his integrity questioned, he had to admit that he'd be suspicious too, if the shoe was on the other foot. He nodded. "I understand where you're coming from. I'm still as shocked as you are. And, for the record, I assure you that in no way did I manipulate or coerce Margaret into writing me into her will."

There was silence for a long minute as Jarryd stared at the two. They didn't meet his eyes.

"Well, I better go," he said finally, feeling like he'd made his point. "Thank you both for taking the time to see me."

"Sure," Olivia said with a smile, escorting him to the door while Elliot gave him a lazy goodbye wave.

"Please excuse my son, Jarryd," Olivia said as they stopped by the elevators. "I'll talk to him. He was wrong to insinuate that you're dishonest."

"Thank you. I appreciate that. See you again soon." He followed Olivia with his eyes as she walked back to the meeting room. He might own half of the company, but if he happened to demand changes, there'd be a stalemate if Olivia and Elliot both disagreed with him. Not that he saw any reason to go against the two at this point in time, but he was pleased that Olivia didn't seem to have any animosity towards him.

He switched his attention to the indicators that flashed the levels the lifts were currently on, and he felt the need to go to the bathroom before leaving the building. He walked to Lilah's desk. "Excuse me, could you tell me where the men's room is on this floor?"

The woman flashed him a simpering smile. "I think you should use the executive restrooms, Mr. Westbourne. It's right next to Boardroom One, two doors down from the meeting room you've just been in."

"Thank you." He was surprised that the receptionist appeared to know his status as the leading shareholder of the company.

He turned to the corridor and was about to pass the meeting room where he'd met with Olivia and Elliot when he heard Olivia's raised voice—muffled but clear behind the closed door.

"All I'm asking is for you to be nice to him! Is that too much to ask?"

Jarryd couldn't help but stop in his tracks. Were they talking about him?

"I can't stand the man!" Elliot said, his voice just as loud. "And who knows? I just might annoy the hell out of him enough that he'll sell his shares so he won't have to deal with me anymore."

"That's stupid thinking. He might want to annoy you back and keep the shares. Just let me deal with him alone next time. We don't want him sticking his nose in our business."

The hairs on Jarryd's neck rose. He looked around, ensuring there was no one about, and leaned closer to the door as Olivia and Elliot's voices calmed down.

"Fine," Elliot said. "You deal with the idiot. Patrick obviously doesn't want to tarnish his wholesome image."

Jarryd scowled. What the hell did that mean? Were the two in cahoots with Patrick in Patrick's mission to strip him of his inheritance?

He grabbed the doorknob, intent on confronting mother and son.

"Fucking Grant Ace is another problem," Elliot said. "We have to stop them."

Jarryd froze.

"Be careful what you say out loud," Olivia said, her tone steely.

"Sure, Mother," Elliot said with sarcasm. "Anyway, I'm late for a staff meeting. I'll see you later."

Jarryd hurried to the next room, instinct telling him not to get caught.

Bloody hell. Olivia and Elliot seemed to be doing something dodgy. And it involved him, Patrick and the Grants.

*****

"I don't know, Jarryd," Carl said, stroking his jaw in contemplation. "What you heard might have sounded suspicious, but there's nothing concrete about any of it. They do want your shares, so it's understandable that Olivia wants Elliot to be nice to you so you'll cooperate. As for mentioning Patrick's name, well, they obviously know of his conflict with you. Maybe what Elliot said was just an observation on his part about Patrick's reluctance to take a definitive step against you. And their comment about Grant Ace could simply mean they want to stop them winning Well of Brilliance by outbidding them."

Jarryd let out a heavy sigh. He'd been running Olivia and Elliot's conversation over and over in his head in the last couple of days, and he knew Carl was right. Nothing he'd heard warranted putting a noose around Olivia's and Elliot's necks. But his instinct insisted it wasn't all innocent. "I know there's not much to go on, but I think we need to check up on it. I'll hate myself if I just sit and wait, knowing they might be planning something detrimental against me and the Grants."

"You want Bray Hayden to sniff around?"

"That's a good idea."

Carl called the private investigator and put him on speaker. Jarryd got him up to speed.

"No problem," Bray said. "But you also have a good chance of picking up something of substance, Jarryd.

You have a reason to keep meeting with Olivia and Elliot and questioning them about things. And you're still friends with Marilyn Grant, right? You can do some subtle poking around without revealing your secrets to her. She might let it slip that her parents have known enemies, for example. Then we'd have something to sink our teeth into."

Jarryd stared at Carl's phone. Bray was right. He did have the opportunity to get some good information. Unfortunately, this was further reason why he couldn't tell Marilyn and her parents about Margaret and his inheritance.

No way they'd believe he was only interested in helping Grant Ace if he told them he owned fifty percent of Greeves Minerals. Given their past experience with Marilyn's deceitful ex-boyfriend, they'd most likely think he only wanted them to back off as Greeves Minerals' competition for Well of Brilliance. That would hurt Marilyn so much.

He let out a heavy breath. As far as he could see, his only acceptable option was to keep them in the dark until he had something concrete to share with them. And he had to be careful not to arouse their suspicions while he tried to draw out some information. If there was anything he didn't want to lose, it was Marilyn's trust.

CHAPTER NINE

Marilyn hurried to the coffee shop where she'd agreed to meet Jarryd for lunch, the several bags she was carrying making it hard for her to walk as fast as she wanted. She hated making him wait, but selecting outfits for the various Christmas parties she needed to attend had taken longer than expected. And frankly, shopping was one of her favourite things to do.

She entered the café and immediately spotted Jarryd sitting at a table near the window, playing with his phone and looking oh so handsome.

Her lips curved up happily. Heck, she could even feel her heart smile. They'd both been so busy trying to get things done before the holidays that they hadn't had time to sleep together during the weekdays. Fortunately, they'd be spending another weekend together.

She navigated her way through the aisles, careful not to annoy people sitting at their tables with her bags.

Jarryd looked up when she reached him, his grin blinding.

"Hi, babe," he said, standing up to give her a peck on the lips.

"Hi. Sorry I'm late. I had to finish my shopping since I won't have any other free time before the parties."

She placed the bags under their table as she sat down in the chair next to him.

"Looks like you bought the whole store," Jarryd joked. "What did you get?"

She took out a black-and-gold V-neck sheath dress from its carry bag. "What do you think of this? This is what I plan to wear to the Christmas Eve party my parents are hosting at their place."

Jarryd's gaze went to her cleavage, then back to the dress, then back again to the valley between her breasts. His forehead creased and his lips pursed.

"It does show a little skin," she said, surprised by his expression. "I thought you liked my boobs."

"Of course I do. But I don't relish the thought of having to poke out other guys' eyes at your parents' party."

Marilyn raised her brows. "What?"

"Which of your exes are going to be attending? You said before that you've gone out with sons of your parents' friends."

She suppressed her smile at his jealous tone. "I only dated a couple of them *a long time* ago. I wasn't at all serious with them or them with me."

Jarryd leaned close to her, his gaze intense. "I still want to be introduced to them."

"Why?"

"So I can hammer it into their heads that you're mine now."

She grinned, loving that he was possessive of her. "No need to bring anything from your toolbox. One of them is already happily married and the other one is Simon—and you already know Simon."

Jarryd narrowed his eyes.

"Don't tell me you're jealous of Simon. You know he's one of my best friends."

"He wants to get in your panties," he said with a low growl.

She laughed, remembering Simon's joke at Lexie and Rick's place. "He does not. You know how he loves to tease. And as if I'd want to sleep with him. He's like a brother to me."

That seemed to placate Jarryd. He kissed her lips and smiled at her. "I was thinking of getting a new suit today for your parents' party, but I've changed my mind. I think I'll get it on Wednesday or Thursday instead."

She gasped delightedly. "I didn't know you planned to go shopping today. We can get it after lunch."

"Nah."

"Why not?"

"I'd rather we go back to your place."

"But why? This is the perfect time to get it. I really don't mind. I can help you chose, since you seem to hate shopping so much."

Jarryd snorted, and his actual intention dawned on her.

"Tell you what," Marilyn said coquettishly, running a finger on his arm. "You can imprison me in my bedroom all weekend…"

Jarryd's nostrils flared as he sucked in a deep breath.

"If we get your suit after lunch."

Jarryd groaned, slumping back in his chair.

"I'll help you choose," she said pleadingly.

"Okay, then," he said resignedly.

She clapped her hands.

Jarryd chuckled. "So what else have you got here?" He bent down to check out her other purchases.

She bit her lip. Not that she didn't want Jarryd to snoop, but the rest of the items were a lot pricier than the dress she'd shown him.

She knew Jarryd wouldn't have a problem mingling with people who wore outfits costlier than his. Those things didn't bother him. But she had a feeling he would extend himself for *her*. While he seemed to be doing well in his business now, she assumed he couldn't afford to fork out the kind of money her parents' circle spent on mere clothes. She'd deliberately bought a dress that would go with the black suit and gold tie he'd worn before, so he wouldn't need to get a new outfit. She hadn't realised he was planning on going shopping for one anyway.

Jarryd's eyebrows shot up as he peered inside one of the shopping bags. He must have seen the price tag.

"They were on sale," she said hurriedly.

Jarryd cocked his head. "Don't you get discounts since your family owns the shopping centre?"

Marilyn let out a laugh. "No. Although they'd probably give me a good one if they knew who I am."

"Hey, you could lose that anonymity if you went on *Biz Q&A*."

"I know," she said with a sigh. Jarryd had been subtly discouraging her to appear on the show. He probably didn't like the idea of being dragged into the spotlight for being her boyfriend.

Fortunately, Patrick was agreeable to her delaying her decision until mid-January. That would be the time the

Tramwells would be announcing which offer they'd accepted. There wasn't much motivation for her to appear on *Biz Q&A* if they weren't successful in acquiring Well of Brilliance, which she'd told her parents she would head if Grant Ace became its new owners.

"Wow, look at this," Jarryd said, whistling as he held up her new Hermès evening bag.

She felt heat rush to her face.

"Are you blushing?"

"Um… well… I don't usually spend this much money on myself in one day. But I have to go to this function attended by—"

"Hey." Jarryd reached out for her hand to silence her. "Why are you justifying yourself to me?"

She stared into his eyes. "I don't want you to think I'm high-maintenance."

Jarryd frowned. "As if I don't already know you're *not*."

"I don't want you thinking that these are the kinds of gifts you have to top to impress me."

Jarryd exhaled loudly, shaking his head. "Marilyn, please don't make excuses for the fact that you can afford these things. I don't care."

She sighed her relief. "Okay."

"Good," Jarryd said, smiling at her with clear desire in his eyes as he stroked her thigh under the table. "Let's eat so you can pick my gear for your parents' party, and then we can go back to your place."

Marilyn licked her lips. This beautiful, perfect man couldn't wait to be alone with her. And now she couldn't wait to get the shopping done.

*****

"What do you think?" Jarryd asked, meeting Marilyn's critical eyes in the mirror as she leaned against the frame of the fitting room door.

She shook her head, wrinkling her nose.

"Really? I thought this was good," Jarryd said. Then under his breath he added, "I just wanna go home."

She smirked as she watched him shrug out of the jacket.

The fine-tailored ensemble he'd chosen from the first store he'd spotted did fit him well. But she wanted to buy his new suit for him—from a shop on the ground floor that used exceptional-quality fabric. The cost would be several times the amount of this particular getup, but he'd said not to apologise for what she could afford, hadn't he?

Jarryd unbuttoned the white dress shirt he'd tried on, letting her get a peek at the muscular torso underneath.

She ogled him openly. "Seriously, you're so hot."

She stifled a surprised shriek when Jarryd yanked her inside the fitting room, then locking the door. Goodness, had she really said that out loud?

"I'm hot, alright," Jarryd murmured, crowding her against the wall. "Hot for you since I left your place on Monday morning. Five fucking days is too fucking long to wait to fuck you again."

Moisture rushed to her core at his words. She craved him too. "But the salesperson's just outside," she whispered.

"So what?"

Marilyn playfully slapped his behind.

"I haven't had you for *five long days*," Jarryd rasped, cupping her breast. "You shouldn't try my patience by smacking my ass. Let's just get this suit, then be on our way."

"No, not this one. Also, I think we should get you a new pair of shoes. We can't go home until I'm fully satisfied."

"Ah, why didn't you say so?" Jarryd pressed her flush against him as he ran a hand underneath her skirt. "I'll be more than happy to satisfy you right here."

She giggled as she tried to push him away. Weakly. How could she strongly resist when his burgeoning erection was digging into her belly?

A sound of a throat being cleared came from outside their door, followed by some knocking. "Can I help you in there?" the salesman asked.

"No, thank you. I can manage by myself," Jarryd called out, his naughty fingers reaching her underwear. He groaned softly in her ear when he found her moist.

"Jarryd!" she said in a fervent whisper, squirming to get out of his embrace. This was getting out of hand.

Jarryd nuzzled her neck, his breath hot on her skin as his fingers continued their delicious rubbing against her panties.

Oh, God, Jarryd was losing control—and she wasn't far behind.

"Okay, we won't buy you new shoes," she said, desperately hanging on to a thread of restraint. "Let's go to the shop I have in mind and we'll be done in fifteen minutes, if they have your size. And since you're not buying from here, you really have to get out of these." She tugged at the trousers he was still wearing.

Bad choice of words.

Jarryd quickly took them off and left her gawking at the big bulge covered by his briefs. Well, not completely covered because the thick head of his erection was poking out from the top of the waistband.

Marilyn swallowed, getting more soaked.

Knock, knock, knock. "Do you need a different size? A different style?" the salesman asked loudly.

"No, thanks," she answered, shutting her eyes to regain her self-control.

"Fifteen minutes at the next shop and that's it," Jarryd murmured authoritatively, putting on his jeans and adjusting himself.

Thank heavens.

Before she got tempted again, she left the change room and let Jarryd get dressed.

She walked outside the store to avoid the sales guy, who must have heard her and Jarryd. Two minutes later, Jarryd was by her side, sliding an arm around her waist.

"Are you sure we need to get my suit today?"

"Yes," she said reluctantly, wanting nothing more than to be in her bed with him. But if she was going to pay, it had to be today.

She took his hand and led him downstairs.

"This is it," she said, stopping in front of one of the best suit shops in Sydney. "Tristan said they're really good."

"Okay," Jarryd said in surprise—or was that dismay?

She was about to ask him not to worry about the cost when Jarryd opened the door and led her inside with a hand on the small of her back.

"Hello," a fifty-something gentleman said cheerfully. "How can I help you?"

"Hi," Jarryd answered. "My girlfriend said that I'm to get my suit here. Apparently, you're highly recommended by her cousin."

The man gave Marilyn a big smile. "Great! May I ask who this cousin is?"

"Tristan Grant."

"Ah, yes, Mr. Grant. He was last here two months ago, I think. I'm Taylor, the tailor."

"Ah, so you're the famous Taylor the Tailor," Marilyn said with a grin. "I'm Marilyn and this is Jarryd."

"Good to meet you both. Are you looking for a bespoke?" Taylor asked Jarryd.

"I actually need one before Christmas Eve, so I don't think there's enough time for that?" Jarryd said.

Taylor put on an apologetic face. "No, one month is our current turnaround time for a bespoke. But we have superbly crafted ready-to-wear suits here. We can make the necessary alterations and have it ready for you by Friday."

"That'll be perfect. Do you want to choose for me, honey?"

Marilyn happily nodded and followed Taylor to the racks of luxurious men's suits. She focused on those that felt lightweight and supple—perfect for summer—and found Jarryd a light grey one to try on. She also chose a white dress shirt and a navy-blue grenadine tie to go with it.

"Come with me inside," Jarryd whispered as Taylor took the items to the fitting room.

"No, or we might not finish here in fifteen minutes."

Jarryd pouted, trudging to the change room.

She chuckled, tempted to pinch his tight ass, but refrained. Taylor knew members of her family, so she better be on her best behaviour.

The suit, incredibly enough, was a perfect fit for Jarryd. Even Taylor, with his exacting standards, was happy not to make a single alteration.

"This looks pretty good, hey, babe?" Jarryd said, checking himself from different angles.

"Yes. You look so handsome," she said with a swooning sigh.

Jarryd grinned.

"And I know just the dress to wear with this," she said. "It's navy blue like your tie, with a light grey sash belt. It's absolutely gorgeous. I've already tried it on earlier, so I'll only need to pay for it." That navy-blue number had been her first choice. But since Jarryd was bound to see the price tag, she hadn't bought it.

"So why didn't you get it earlier?"

"Because... I like the black-and-gold dress too. But that other dress would match this ensemble better. We can look like a cute couple who planned our get-ups together."

"Hm, I like the sound of that. Okay. Two minutes to get that dress, then."

"Five. We have to go back up. And depends on how busy they are." She giggled as her super-hot boyfriend rolled his eyes.

Jarryd got changed and she whispered to Taylor. "I want to get Jarryd's outfit as a gift for him. Can I pay now while he's getting ready?"

"Of course."

Marilyn took a deep breath, hoping Jarryd wouldn't mind.

She'd just finished paying when Jarryd came out of the fitting room. Taylor took the garments from him and went to pack them.

"Hey." She wrapped her arms around Jarryd's waist. "This is my Christmas gift to you."

Jarryd frowned.

"I already paid for it," she said, flashing him an impish smile and hoping it would make him accept her present without a fuss.

Jarryd stared at her for a long moment before letting out a harsh sigh. "Are you doing this because you don't think I can pay for it? And did you drag me here because the other guests at your parents' party will be dressed in expensive threads and you want me to blend in with them?"

Oh, no. The last thing she wanted was for Jarryd to feel he wasn't good enough as he was.

CHAPTER TEN

Guilt hit Jarryd at the anxiety that had sprung into Marilyn's eyes. He wasn't angry at her for giving him a gift, but he was annoyed that she wasn't up front in saying that the suit he'd originally chosen wasn't suitable for her folks' party—that she wanted him to wear one that cost several thousand dollars. Skirting around the issue just made him feel small, even though he could easily manage to pay for it himself.

But did he have the right to make her feel bad when he couldn't divulge to her the truth about his financial status?

Marilyn gave him a peck on the lips, her gaze pleading. "You told me not to apologise for what I can afford. I want to buy this for you, so don't go backing away from your words now. And for the record, I think you'd look good amongst my parents' guests *whatever you wear*."

"So if I decide to wear that black suit I wore at Carter and Cassie's wedding, you won't mind?"

"Not at all," Marilyn said without hesitation. "The gold tie you wore with it matches my new black-and-gold dress."

Jarryd cocked his head, frowning. "Wait. Is that why you bought that dress and not the navy-blue one you were just gushing about?"

"Yes. I assumed you weren't planning on buying a new outfit just for my parents' party."

He sighed. How could he remain mad at her when she was so sweet?

Marilyn ran her hands on his chest, her lashes fluttering. "But I do love that navy-blue dress and I do love shopping for you. So please accept this gift? *Wholeheartedly?*"

Ah, how could he resist her? He kissed her lips and squeezed her tight. "Okay. Thank you. I do appreciate it very much."

Marilyn grinned at him happily.

His own lips tugged upwards. He could stare at her all day, especially when joy was painted all over her beautiful face. But he wanted to touch her all over too, and they needed to be home for that. He released her to grab all their shopping bags. "Let's go get your dress."

Marilyn led him back to the level that was the domain of high-end designer brands, and she went straight for the shop and the particular rack where the dress she wanted was hanging.

"Hi, I'm back," she said to the saleslady, checking the sizes of the garments and grabbing one. "I'm getting this navy blue."

"Can I see it on you first, babe?" Jarryd asked.

Marilyn glanced at him in surprise. "I thought you were in a hurry to get home."

"Well, I can't wait to see you in it."

"Okay," Marilyn said, squinting her eyes at him as a warning not to follow her into the fitting room.

He gave her a cheery wave, staying where he was near the counter. When she disappeared behind one of the doors, he went to the saleslady. "Hi. I'd like to pay for that dress now, please."

"Oh, sure." The shop assistant took one from the rack and scanned the tag.

His brows rose when the helpful lady told him the price. It was over four thousand dollars. For one dress. Wow. He hadn't even noticed any crystals on it.

He handed his credit card, his brain joining the dots. He could see it clearly now. Marilyn had bought herself the much cheaper black-and-gold dress to go with the black suit and gold tie he already owned. There wasn't anything wrong with that suit whatsoever. But he supposed those in the know could easily tell how much a suit cost just from looking at the fabric.

Marilyn didn't want to outshine him at the party. She planned to dress down for him, not caring what her parents' guests might think.

He bet that as the Grants' daughter, she was usually among the best-dressed people at her folks' events. And yet she wouldn't care if her garb for this coming one was not as high-fashion as per her usual—so that they could be a cute couple who wore "matching" outfits.

God, he loved her.

Yes. He did.

He stilled as the realisation hit him squarely in the chest.

The saleslady finalised the purchase and a full smile formed on his face.

He'd already fallen.

He was already in love with Marilyn.

And damn, he was happy about that.

Jarryd placed his credit card back in his wallet along with the receipt and went to stand outside Marilyn's fitting room, just as she was opening the door.

His mouth hung open. His girlfriend—the woman he loved—was gorgeous in the form-fitting strapless dress. The blue did seem as navy as his tie, and the colour of the sash was close to the light grey shade of his suit.

"I guess that means you like it," Marilyn said, pleased by his expression.

"You look stunning, babe." He leaned in to whisper in her ear. "I can't wait to strip it off you."

"Not until after my parents' Christmas Eve party," Marilyn quipped, patting his cheek.

He slipped an arm around her waist. "Can't you leave it on today? I promise to be careful when I take it off you when we get to your place."

Marilyn shook her head. "I know what you're like when you're excited. You'll ruin this dress."

"I'll buy you another one."

Marilyn chuckled, still shaking her head as she started to close the door of the change room. Then she froze, looking up at him with suspicious eyes. "What do you mean you'll buy me another one?"

"If I ruin it, I'll get you another one."

"But you're not buying *this* one." It was a statement, not a question.

"Too late," he said with a bright smile.

"Jarryd." Dismay dripped from Marilyn's tone.

He cupped her face, all serious now. "Hey, I *wholeheartedly* accepted your gift. I want you to wholeheartedly accept mine now."

Her brows furrowed as her eyes moistened. "You're trying to pay me back."

Oh, hell. Tears? She wasn't playing fair.

"I'm not trying to pay you back. I'm just... wanting to give you an early Christmas present too."

"I shouldn't have bought you that suit," Marilyn muttered.

"I love that suit! Come on. Don't be like this."

"This is too much, Jarryd," she said in a fierce whisper.

"And the suit wasn't?" he asked dryly.

"You know what I mean."

He slowly let out a sigh. "This dress comes in black too and would have matched my black suit at home. Why did you get the black-and-gold dress instead of the black version of this?"

Marilyn huffed. "I don't want money to come between us, so what does it matter?"

"*Exactly.* I don't want money to come between us either. And I *can* afford this, so please don't worry."

"You don't need to buy me this kind of stuff to please me."

"I know. But it *pleases me* to buy you this kind of stuff."

"That's not good use of your money," Marilyn said insistently.

"And it's good use of your money to buy me what you just bought me?"

"Yes."

"Why?"

"Because…" Marilyn swallowed. "Because I have more money than you."

He laughed. If she only knew—

He sobered. She couldn't know yet.

"Look," he said, caressing her cheeks with his thumbs. "We both don't want money to come between us, so let's agree to not discuss money, okay? I promise that I won't spend beyond my means, but only if you promise not to make a big deal of it if I choose to buy you things or pay for our dinners or trips or whatever."

"So you're saying you won't go over the top with presents for me?"

"That's not what I said. I said I promise I won't spend beyond my means."

Marilyn searched his face, trying to understand his statement.

"Come on, babe," he said quietly. "Arguing about this is ridiculous. Let's stop it. Please."

"Okay," Marilyn said with a resigned smile. "I promise to accept whatever you pay for wholeheartedly *if* you promise to only spend what's within your budget. I don't want you getting into any debt, credit card or otherwise, for anything concerning me."

"Deal."

They sealed it with a kiss.

*****

Jarryd sat on the bed and ran his hand on Marilyn's naked back as she lay on her stomach. "Do you want to sleep or do you want me to start heating up the food?"

Marilyn mumbled an answer against the pillow.

"What did you say? You'd rather stay in bed and make love again?" he teased.

Marilyn rolled to her side, her lids droopy even as she grinned. "You're insatiable. I know I said you could imprison me here for the whole weekend, but aren't you going to let me rest?"

He chuckled. "If my memory serves me right, the last two rounds were your idea. We were going to have an afternoon nap, but you seduced me instead. Then we were going to eat our food when it arrived, but you dragged me back to bed."

"The last two rounds might have been my idea, but the five before that have been all yours."

"Five? I thought it was six. Anyway, three of them happened yesterday, so they shouldn't count towards today."

"Are you keeping a daily tally?"

"Just making up for the next few days that I won't see you. I'm not looking forward to missing you like crazy."

Marilyn clasped her hands behind his neck and pulled him down to her. "I have the sweetest boyfriend."

"See? You're doing it again," he said against her lips.

"Doing what again?"

"Seducing me."

"I am not," she said with fake indignation. "I'm just kissing you."

He rolled his eyes. Didn't she have any idea how arousing her kisses were?

Marilyn's tummy grumbled loudly and they both laughed.

"I think I have to feed you first before I make love to you again. Stay here and I'll prepare dinner." He rubbed his nose with hers before pushing himself off the bed.

"Thank you, honey," Marilyn murmured, closing her eyes.

He smiled as he strutted to Marilyn's kitchen. He retrieved three takeaway containers from the fridge and divided the contents into two big bowls before popping the first one in the microwave. Marilyn should enjoy having their Thai dinner in her bed, considering she didn't seem to want to get out of it.

He'd love a snooze too, but he'd wait until it was truly time to sleep. He hadn't been kidding when he'd said he was trying to make up for the one whole week that he wouldn't be spending with her.

Marilyn would be busy with Christmas functions every single weeknight, both for work and for charity. Pity he couldn't accompany her to any of them. He himself had a project that absolutely needed to be finished by Friday—the last working day of the year for Westbourne Constructions before they took a break during the holiday period.

Jarryd hoped that Marilyn could take time off between Christmas and New Year as well. She'd promised she'd try to get urgent things done this week so she could. Once he got her confirmation, he'd book a romantic trip somewhere.

He couldn't wait to spend several days alone with her. It wasn't simply a matter of wanting to—he needed to. The new year would be bringing with it some challenges that would affect their relationship, and he was keen to keep showing her how much she meant to him. He hoped that before the inevitable storm came, she wouldn't have any doubts that his feelings for her were real—that he'd never use her for his own gain or that of Greeves Minerals.

He rubbed his face. He was itching to tell Marilyn everything so that the guilt he'd been carrying around with him would finally go away. But no matter how much he looked at things from all angles, he always ended up with the same conclusion: he couldn't yet, not if he didn't want to take the risk of Marilyn and her parents misunderstanding or, worse, disbelieving him. He'd kept the truth hidden about him co-owning Greeves Minerals for too long after learning about Patrick's invitation for Marilyn to appear on *Biz Q&A* and Grant Ace's bid for Well of Brilliance. Revealing his secrets now would only do more harm than good.

There was still a month to go before the Tramwells would either announce their decision on which offer to accept, or ask more questions regarding the bids. Lorna and Ben Tramwell had already gone on their respective holidays overseas.

That was a blessing. That gave him and Bray time to sniff around and see if Olivia and Elliot were planning something dishonest.

The possibility that Olivia and Elliot were planning to sabotage Grant Ace in the name of Greeves Minerals was giving him sleepless nights. But without any concrete proof, it would be stupid to get any formal investigation going. So far, Olivia had given him nothing except to assure him that she and the Greeves Minerals team were doing their best to win Well of Brilliance. She'd been stonewalling him when it came to how they were handling any moves by the competition. He didn't want to push too hard, though. If Olivia picked up that he suspected something, the more she'd try to cover things up.

And then there were Margaret's wishes. She'd clearly wanted to win Well of Brilliance, having initiated the negotiations to buy it. He hated feeling disloyal to his birth mother and the legacy she'd left him, but if Olivia and Elliot were doing something shady, how could he not fight against it? Margaret would have understood that, wouldn't she?

He exhaled harshly and concentrated on fixing their dinner. There was nothing he could do about any of his problems this weekend, so he would ignore them, which he'd been very good at doing when he was with Marilyn.

He smiled. He bet Marilyn would be asleep when he came back to the bedroom, and he'd have a fun time waking her up.

Ah, he just couldn't get enough of her.

When all the food was heated up, he arranged their dinner bowls on a bed tray and added a glass of water they could share. Then he carried them back to Marilyn's bedroom, his own stomach grumbling from the delicious smells coming from the beef massaman curry, chicken and basil stir-fry, and jasmine rice.

He pushed the door open and found Marilyn sitting up against the headboard, the sheets tucked under her armpits to cover her nakedness and the phone held up against her ear. She smiled when she saw him, but he could tell that whatever conversation she was having with whomever had made her quite angry.

"Is there anything I can do?" Marilyn asked the person on the other end of the line. "Gavin?... Okay, I'll see what I can do."

Jarryd's brows rose. Someone must be in a spot of bother to want to talk to their private detective friend, Gavin Redford.

"I will, Dad," Marilyn said. "See you guys next week at the party. Bye."

Jarryd's heart raced. He placed the tray in the middle of the bed and sat next to Marilyn. "Everything okay?"

Marilyn moved closer to him. "Remember when I said that my parents want to buy a company that they want me to head?"

He nodded, dread lodging in his chest as he guessed what she was about to say.

"Well, the CEO called Dad from the US, where she's having a holiday. Apparently, a contact told her that Grant Ace is only using Well of Brilliance—that's the company we're trying to buy—as leverage to get a better outcome on another deal my parents are trying to secure. The CEO's acquaintance said that Grant Ace is not really serious about Well of Brilliance, and that we would pull out of the negotiations once we finalise the other supposed deal. It's all false, of course, and Dad is furious, especially since the CEO refused to name her acquaintance who'd passed on the accusations."

So it had begun. He let out a calming breath before speaking. "I heard you mention Gavin."

"Yeah. After Dad convinced the Well of Brilliance CEO that what she'd heard has no basis to it, she agreed to keep considering Grant Ace's bid. But, Dad being Dad, he wants to get to the bottom of the fake rumour. He'd asked me to talk to Gavin since Gavin's someone he knows he can trust."

Jarryd gulped involuntarily. *Trust.* That word just pounded his guilt back into him.

"Dad did say to wait until after the holidays before I mention it to Gavin. Since the CEO accepted his explanation, it's not urgent. But he still wants to find out who started it all."

He took a deep breath. He had to tell her now. "Okay, let's talk about this," he said, steeling himself for this conversation.

But Marilyn shook her head vigorously. "No, let's not. I'm so overloaded with work that I don't want to think about this right now. I just want to relax this weekend. Come Monday, I'll be having one of my most hectic weeks of the year trying to get everything done before the Christmas break. The time for this problem is after New Year's."

"Okay," he said, relieved and glad for the reprieve. He still had time to think about what to do next. But he was in deeper trouble now that Marilyn had shared this issue with him.

He *had* to be the one to confess to Marilyn and the Grants *before* they discovered his secrets. How and when he was going to do that, he had absolutely no idea.

CHAPTER ELEVEN

Marilyn checked her watch for the umpteenth time, wondering why Jarryd was late. He was usually never late for their dates.

It wasn't that they'd agreed on a specific time he was supposed to arrive today. But when she'd asked for him to come early so they could have lunch together before they got ready for her parents' Christmas Eve party tonight, she assumed he'd be here at—well, no later than eleven?

She rolled her eyes at herself. It was just that she missed him so much. With the last week being one of the busiest times of the year for the both of them, she couldn't wait to be with him again.

Fortunately, she was taking time off between Christmas and New Year's. She normally worked through those days as it was the best period to get things done without interruptions, but Jarryd had been persuading her to take a break for the next two weeks. He didn't have to say it, but she knew he was planning on taking her on a trip somewhere. Of course she wouldn't want to miss that!

She should start preparing their roast beef sandwiches for lunch, just for something to do to while the time away. She opened the fridge, and the doorbell rang.

Yay, he was here! Was it too early in their relationship to give each other keys to their places?

She groaned, shaking her head at herself as she hastened to answer the door. Goodness, what had Jarryd fed her that she was so head over heels?

She was aware of her big smile when she opened the door. "Hi."

"Hi," Jarryd answered, leaning in to kiss her lips. "Missed you," he murmured.

Her heart sang. "Missed you too."

"Can I hang this in your bedroom?" Jarryd held up his suit bag.

"Of course. I'll be in the kitchen making our lunch."

Jarryd frowned at her.

"What?"

"We didn't see each other for a week and all you can think of is lunch?"

She grinned. "It's roast beef sandwiches. One of your favourites."

Jarryd curved an arm around her waist. "But I've been looking forward to my fill of Marilyn Grant."

"Fine," she said, pretending to be stern. "But you only have two hours to feast on me."

Jarryd bent down and lifted her over his shoulder. "Two hours is nowhere near enough, but I'll take it."

She giggled, slapping his sexy ass from her upside-down position as he took her to the bedroom. Her hand hit something like a box in Jarryd's back pocket. She braced herself to see what it was.

Her own bottom felt a whack.

"Hey, don't look at it," Jarryd warned.

"Why not?" She tried again and glimpsed something blue. A distinctive Tiffany & Co blue. Her breathing shallowed. Had Jarryd bought her a Christmas gift?

"Naughty girl," Jarryd said as he put her down on the foot of her bed and went to her en suite to hang his suit bag.

She followed him with her eyes. "What is it?"

"It's my suit," he quipped.

"No. That thing in your back pocket."

Jarryd sighed, walking back to her. "It was supposed to be a surprise for tomorrow."

She gazed at him in dismay.

"What's that look for?" he asked with a frown.

"You already bought me a Christmas present—the navy-blue dress I'm wearing tonight."

"So? I wanted to get you something else."

"Jarryd…" Damn, she hadn't got him anything else because she was afraid he might spend more on her if she did. Turned out he had, anyway.

"You promised," Jarryd said accusingly.

"What?"

"You promised you'll accept whatever I give you *wholeheartedly.*"

"And did you keep your end of the bargain?"

"Yes, I did," Jarryd said quietly. "Marilyn, I appreciate you being concerned about my financial well-being, but please stop questioning everything I give you. This can't keep going on. It's going to ruin our pleasure when giving each other gifts."

Guilt swamped her. "Okay. I'm sorry. I just didn't want you overextending yourself for me."

"All I'm asking you is to not question my decision on the things I want to give you."

She curved her arms around his neck. "You're right. I'm sorry. Please forgive me?"

Jarryd pulled her closer, a grin on his face. "Only if you kiss me."

She gave him a quick peck on the lips. "Now can I have my present?"

"It's not Christmas yet."

"But what if I want to wear it tonight?"

"How do you know it's something wearable?"

"It's in a Tiffany box," she said pointedly.

Jarryd rolled his eyes, chuckling. "You'll have to wait till tomorrow. And I'm sure you've already planned your accessories for tonight."

She had, but she'd rather wear whatever Jarryd had bought for her, even if it wasn't a perfect match for her dress. She wanted him to know she was proud of whatever he'd given her. She batted her eyelashes at him. "Pretty please?"

"As if that would work," Jarryd muttered, but took the box out of his back pocket and handed it to her. "Merry Christmas, honey."

She took it from him, seeing the apprehension that suddenly lined his face. Was he worried she wouldn't like it?

She untied the bow and carefully lifted the lid. Her mouth dropped open. A platinum heart lock pendant with round brilliant diamonds glittered inside the box. Now she knew why he looked nervous. This necklace would be more than double the price of her navy-blue dress. Easily.

Jarryd cupped her face. "My heart, it's yours," he whispered.

She smiled, her eyes moistening. "I accept. *Wholeheartedly*. Thank you."

Jarryd took a deep breath, his face clearing.

"This is perfect for my dress." She lifted the chain out of the box to better admire it.

"Marilyn," Jarryd said softly.

She glanced up at him. "Yes?"

"I love you."

Her heart skipped. And so did she, launching herself at Jarryd. "I love you too."

Laughter rumbled out of Jarryd's throat as they kissed passionately, their lips confirming the declaration they'd just made.

She was in love. And the man she was crazy about loved her back. It had finally happened for her. Wow.

"I also have another present for you," she murmured against his lips.

"You do?"

"Uh-huh. It's not something I bought, but it's something of mine that I want you to have. I was just thinking about it when you arrived and it's a perfect complement for what you gave me." She took her arms from around his neck to reinspect her new necklace, touching the keyhole design on the heart pendant.

"Are you gonna give it to me now?"

With a smile, she went to her dresser and grabbed her spare set of house keys from the bottom drawer. Then she walked back to Jarryd and placed them in his hand.

The awe on Jarryd's face told her it was the perfect gift. He took her back in his arms and squeezed her tight. "Thank you. I better get my apartment keys duplicated for you too."

"Okay," she said with a grin.

Jarryd took the Tiffany & Co. box from her and placed it on her nightstand together with the keys she'd given him. Then he ran his hands along her sides and up her chest to cup her breasts. "Now I want to start my two-hour feast."

Her nipples instantly pebbled at the touch of his fingers, and moisture started to pool at the apex between her legs.

"Did you miss me?" Jarryd asked as he lifted her top over her head.

"Yes."

"These do look like they missed me." He rolled her nipples between his thumbs and forefingers.

A little moan was her answer.

Jarryd continued to undress her, his mouth following his hands wherever they roamed her body. Soon she was naked before him, shivering from anticipation when Jarryd took a few seconds to do nothing but simply stare.

Marilyn was tingling all over, every nerve ending in her body focused only on the man standing before her, the love bursting in her chest magnifying the desire zinging in her veins.

How could Jarryd arouse feelings in her that no one else had ever managed to stir?

Jarryd teased her nipples with his tongue, then continued kissing his way down her body. Kneeling in front of her, he parted her pussy lips, revealing to him her swollen nub eager for his attention.

Jarryd didn't disappoint. He poked out his tongue and licked her slowly with its tip, then closed his lips on her clit, sucking gently.

She cried, her legs trembling. She braced herself against his shoulders arching her hips against him wantonly.

"You want more, huh?" Jarryd mumbled, kneading her butt while he continued to lave her nub. "I love it when you want more."

"Yes, more," she said shamelessly. "I always want more with you."

With a groan, Jarryd got to his feet and held her against him in a tight embrace, his mouth seeking hers. Then before she knew it, he had her lying in bed, her ass at the edge and her legs dangling to the floor. He parted her thighs and knelt in between.

"I love that you're soaking for me," Jarryd rasped before burying his tongue in her slit.

"Jarryd!"

"Tell me, baby. I wanna hear it."

She grabbed a fistful of his hair. "More, please."

With a delighted growl, Jarryd licked his way up to her clit, pushing two fingers into her wet heat. Tirelessly, he pleasured her with his mouth and fingers, while all she could do was absorb all he was giving her, her release building up and up.

"Can't wait to be inside this delicious pussy," Jarryd murmured as he continued to lick, suck and stroke.

"Then do it now," she gasped. "Make me come with your cock."

"Ah, you're such a temptress." Jarryd stood up abruptly and hastily took off his clothes.

But she wanted to return the favour first. Scrambling to a sitting position, she pulled Jarryd close so that his erection was right in front of her face. She tasted the dew that formed at the tip before running her tongue on its velvety length. Then, while tugging him at the base, she put him in her mouth.

Jarryd groaned.

"By the way... I have... *another* present... for you," Marilyn said in between sucks.

"All I want is you, babe," Jarryd said breathlessly, running a gentle hand on her bobbing head.

She looked up at him. "This present is connected to that."

"What is it?"

She twirled her tongue on the head of his erection as she cupped his balls. "I'm on the pill. You can ditch the condom."

Jarryd's mouth dropped open. Then he was hauling her back on the bed and eagerly settling himself between her legs. "I want inside here right now," he grunted, inserting his hardness into her welcoming channel.

Her giggle turned into moans as Jarryd pushed himself to the hilt, moving in and out of her. Slowly. Steadily. Purposefully.

Their eyes locked, watching the play of desire and pleasure in each other's faces as they climbed the crest together.

"I love you," she whispered, grabbing his behind to urge him to move faster as her hips undulated to meet his in perfect synchrony.

Jarryd pressed his mouth to hers, kissing her fervently as he drove in deeper, harder. "Say it again," he ordered, adjusting his thrusts so he was hitting her clit with every move.

She gasped, her whole body tensing. "I love you," she cried as her body clamped hard around his cock over and over.

"Ahh, I love you," Jarryd said through gritted teeth, driving into her with abandon, his face contorted with pleasure. Then he stilled for a beat before he yelled in ecstasy, erupting inside her, filling her with his come.

*****

Marilyn stared at herself in the full-length mirror in her bedroom as Jarryd stood behind her, clasping her new necklace around her neck.

There were both fully dressed—she in her strapless navy-blue dress and grey sash, and Jarryd in his fabulous light grey suit and navy-blue tie.

"There," Jarryd said, kissing her bare shoulder when he finished, then standing beside her in front of the mirror. "We do look like a cute couple, don't we?"

"We sure do," she said, putting an arm around his waist. "I can't wait to introduce you to our family friends tonight."

Jarryd beamed at her. "Speaking of tonight, will I be the only one attending your folks' party for the first time?"

"No. There'll be around a dozen or so who are not regular invitees. They're acquaintances of my parents who currently have business dealings with Grant Ace. For some of them, it would be their first time attending. And unless they become really strong business partners, they might not get invited again in the future, simply because my parents try to limit the head count to one hundred."

"Apart from some of our friends, would I know any of the guests?"

She pursed her lips in thought. "I don't think so."

"Patrick O'Neill hasn't changed his mind about not coming, has he?" Jarryd said in a teasing voice. "I'm surprised he didn't move mountains so he could come, especially since he seems to be such a big fan of you Grants, having asked all of you to join him on his show."

Marilyn laughed. "Apparently, he couldn't get out of his family commitments in Brisbane. Mum said he was really keen on going. If he weren't out of town, he most definitely would be there tonight."

"There's next year for him, I suppose."

"That's not guaranteed. Depends on his relationship with Grant Ace next year. He's not a close business associate."

"Well, I'll keep it in mind to show your parents how good I am to you so I make it on the invite list again next year," Jarryd quipped.

She laughed, thrilled that he was already assuming they'd still be together in a year's time. She hoped so too. She twined her fingers with his. "Let's go?"

Jarryd nodded and they walked to her garage. It was Jarryd's idea to use her Mercedes-Benz, jokingly saying that his four-year-old Toyota Camry would stand out like a sore thumb amongst the luxury vehicles that would be parking outside the Grants' house tonight. She'd told him it didn't matter, but Jarryd had been adamant, saying that their "matching" outfits deserved to be transported in her car rather than his.

She wasn't happy that Jarryd thought he had to keep up appearances for her sake, but she let the matter rest. There'd be another time and place where she could assure him that there was not a single thing he needed to change about himself to fit into her life.

Her parents' street was still empty of cars parked on the street when they got there. It was perfect, because she wanted Jarryd to feel settled and relaxed before the other guests arrived. Fortunately, their close friends would be attending tonight. She was bursting to tell all of them about her and Jarryd. The girls had promised they'd drag their men to the party early so they could have a good chat before they'd have to mingle with the others and talk shop.

Gosh, she felt like a giddy woman excited at falling in love for the first time. Well, she guessed she had fallen in *true* love for the first time. She certainly hadn't felt this strongly for anyone else before.

But more than anything, one fact was making her happy like nothing else had ever had.

Jarryd loved her. They were in love *with each other* and she was glad he'd be by her side as her date tonight.

It was only the second time she'd taken a date to her parents' Christmas Eve party—the first time being with that betraying bastard whose name she didn't even want to remember.

And Jarryd was bound to deter a guy who'd been hassling her for dates. She hadn't told Jarryd about him, hoping he wouldn't be attending tonight. But she'd seen his name on the guest list her mum had shown her, and he was coming with his mother.

Marilyn was surprised that her parents had invited Elliot Greeves and his mother Olivia to the party for the first time.

Well, her dad did believe in making friends with the competition. He'd always thought that if things ever go sour, there was less chance of people wanting to vent their anger in the public arena if friendships were established in the first place.

He had a point. Grant Ace had been in some fierce battle with other companies for one reason or another, but the disputes had remained in the boardrooms. Her parents—her dad, in particular—were great at separating the individual entity from the corporate entity. That was a big reason why Grant Ace had managed to avoid the unwanted spotlight for the most part.

Her father's philosophy must have rubbed off on Elliot. The persistent man—who she'd met for the first time at a charity event a few months ago—hadn't backed off asking her out even when Grant Ace had made a bid for Well of Brilliance against Greeves Minerals. Unfortunately, Elliot hadn't taken the hint from her constant refusal.

Well, Elliot would know tonight that she was well and truly taken. She might even introduce Jarryd to him the moment he turned up at the party.

CHAPTER TWELVE

Jarryd felt excited as he and Marilyn walked up the path to the Grants' house. The front garden looked festive, with blinking fairy lights draped around trees and potted plants. Big colourful lightbulbs lined the eaves of the Federation mansion.

He was glad they were early. He'd get the chance to chat with Marilyn's parents before they got busy entertaining other people. After he and Marilyn had said *I love you* to each other for the first time, he also wanted to deepen his relationship with Barry and Alice.

At least he didn't have to worry about Patrick O'Neill being at the party. That was a huge relief. He'd thought he'd have to talk to the man and make threats and promises so Patrick would keep his mouth shut about their conflict. Lucky there was no need for that.

"Your parents aren't expecting you to stay overnight, are they?" he asked Marilyn.

"They probably are. I usually do every year because I tend to have a few glasses of wine. Mum's big on me not driving after I've been drinking. And I'm sure she'd worry about you too. Don't be surprised if she persuades us both to stay overnight."

"But if I stayed here too, they'd probably get me to sleep in one of the guest bedrooms, right?"

"My parents are pretty open-minded. I'm sure they won't mind if you stay with me in my old bedroom, especially since I'm *twenty-eight* and you're *thirty-one*. Besides, they like you already."

"Who changes the bedsheets?" he whispered in her ear.

Marilyn chuckled. "Bea, the housekeeper."

"Good." There were bound to be a few wet spots. He'd hate for Barry and Alice to notice those.

"We can't make a noise, though," Marilyn said.

"Okay."

Marilyn snorted.

He was going to tease her that she was the one who was loud in bed when Alice and Barry appeared at the front door to greet them. To his delight, even Barry gave him a hug hello.

"Oh, don't you look beautiful and handsome in your outfits," Alice said.

"Marilyn obviously dragged Jarryd around the shops," Barry quipped.

"She sure did," Jarryd said cheerily. "And she chose this suit for me. She has great taste."

Barry looked him up and down. "Nice," the older man said, clearly appreciating his clothing.

"This is pretty," Alice murmured, touching Marilyn's heart lock pendant and leaning in for a closer look.

"It's Jarryd's Christmas present to me," Marilyn said a tad shyly.

"It's beautiful. You have good taste too, Jarryd," Alice said with a wide smile, with Barry nodding his acknowledgement.

"Thank you," Jarryd replied. He didn't need the Grants' approval, but he was glad that they were continuing to show him they weren't bothered by the fact that he "couldn't afford" to give Marilyn what she was accustomed to. Clearly, all they wanted was for Marilyn to be happy with her choice of boyfriend.

"Why don't you two come with me while I check that everything's in place before the guests arrive," Alice said. "Barry will man the door."

Jarryd happily followed Alice and Marilyn through the house and noticed a tall Christmas tree standing proudly in the formal living room. There were stacks of large and small boxes sitting underneath it. He wondered if they were real gifts or just decorations.

He hadn't bought Marilyn's parents anything. The Grants didn't want gifts for themselves. Instead, they'd requested their guests to donate to one of the five charities they'd mentioned in their invitation. He'd donated twice to each of them, first under his name, and second as an anonymous donor for much larger amounts.

The festive decor flowed through the whole property, with more fairy lights and lanterns in the shape of stars dotting the large back garden.

The caterers were finishing setting up food trays on top of two extra-long buffet tables. He inhaled deeply, letting the aroma reach his nostrils, and his mouth watered instantly.

"It smells good here," he murmured to Marilyn. "I'm getting hungry."

"Me too, considering we hardly ate lunch."

He grinned at her.

"Didn't you two have lunch?" Alice interjected. "Why don't you have something now? No sense waiting for everyone to arrive if you're hungry."

"Okay," Marilyn said, taking his hand and dragging him to one of the buffet tables, her cheeks reddening.

He chuckled at Marilyn's attempt to hide her embarrassment from her mother. "What's with the blush, babe?"

"You think I can tell my mother I didn't eat much because I was too busy having sex?" she whispered.

"Oh, yeah," he said, as if he'd just remembered what they'd done earlier in the day. "Especially when you were supposed to eat roast beef, but preferred my beef instead."

Marilyn pinched his side. "That is so bad!"

He laughed out loud, pulling her to him and kissing her temple.

"Hey, look who's here," a male voice called out.

Lucas and Jade were walking hand in hand towards them, both grinning from ear to ear.

"Good to see you guys hugging and kissing rather than avoiding each other," Lucas teased. "What happened?"

"What happened?" Jade said to her husband. "Isn't it obvious?"

"Well, I never got to finish my conversation with Jarryd at Rick and Lexie's," Lucas drawled. "But I'm glad you guys sorted it out."

"Jarryd decided that we *did* have enough spark after all," Marilyn joked, glancing at him.

Jarryd squeezed Marilyn tight, remembering how hurt she'd been at his words. "Turns out I can be a big moron sometimes."

"Hey, Jade," Marilyn said. "Wanna have a girlie chat before I get busy playing co-hostess?"

"Yes! Cassie and Carter and Erin and Brad are here now too. We saw them parking outside."

Marilyn grabbed a piece of sushi and led Jade away, the two women giving them a wave.

"Hey, what about me?" Lucas called out.

"Jarryd will fill you in," Marilyn said.

Jarryd chuckled. "I wonder what gets added in a girls-only talk that they don't want to share with us."

"Who knows," Lucas said. "Anyway, I'm dying to know your story. How about you start now before we get interrupted again?"

"Fine," he said with a laugh.

He told Lucas what he'd told Marilyn, pausing when Carter and Brad joined them and starting again from the beginning. His buddies were teasing him about staying overnight at the Grants' when the girls appeared by their side.

"Excuse me, guys," Marilyn said, linking her arms with his. "I need to show off my boyfriend to someone."

"Okay," Brad said. "You might be interested to know that he only said he was a moron about five times."

Jarryd laughed. "Well, I was. I'm just glad Marilyn has forgiven me."

"Because you're so hot," Marilyn said teasingly, leading him away from their friends and towards the house. "I need to introduce you to someone who keeps asking me out and wouldn't take the hint even though I keep declining his invitations."

He frowned. "You haven't mentioned guys hassling you for a date before."

"I keep forgetting. It's not like they're at the forefront of my mind when I'm with you."

He slipped an arm around her waist. "You say the sweetest things."

"It's true," Marilyn said with a shrug. "Anyway, his name's Elliot Greeves, the COO of Greeves Minerals. He just arrived with his mother Olivia, the CEO. They're a bit early."

Jarryd stumbled at the steps leading back into the house, catching himself in time before he fell flat on his face.

"You okay?"

"Uh… yeah. Um, can I go to the bathroom first?"

"Sure. Use my en suite upstairs if you like. More private."

"Okay. Haven't you told this Elliot guy about me before?"

"No. The last time he asked me out, he did it via email, inviting me to some show at the Opera House. It seemed funny to reply with 'leave me alone, I have a boyfriend.' Anyway, he's not annoying, just persistent."

"Right. Okay, I'll be back. In the meantime, avoid Elliot."

Marilyn chuckled. "I will."

Jarryd made his way upstairs, his heart galloping and sweat beading all over his body.

Elliot and Olivia were here? He'd casually asked Olivia what she and Elliot were doing for both Christmas Eve and Christmas Day. Olivia had said they were having a quiet Christmas Eve, then celebrating with her sister's family the next day.

Well, he supposed they'd had a last-minute change of plans and decided to come to this party. Why in the hell had it not occurred to him that they might be on the guest list? There he was, worrying about Patrick and completely forgetting about Elliot and Olivia. Just because they were competing with the Grants for Well of Brilliance didn't mean they weren't friends with Marilyn's parents.

God, he really was an absolute idiot. What was he going to do now?

He went into Marilyn's old bedroom and closed the door. He slumped on her bed and buried his face in his hands.

Could he talk to the two and ask them to keep his secret from Marilyn and her parents?

But Elliot hated his guts. And the man was also after Marilyn. Could he really trust Elliot to help handle the situation delicately, even if Elliot agreed to play along with him?

Argh! Perhaps he should just tell Marilyn all about it—right now, before Elliot had a chance to.

She'd understand, right? She loved him and she knew that he loved her. Things were different now that they'd confessed their feelings for each other.

He stood up, straightening his body. The time had come to tell Marilyn the truth. It was the worst time and place, but he didn't have a choice.

With a deep breath, he opened the door to find Marilyn.

Only to come face-to-face with a scowling Barry Grant.

"You fucker," Barry said in a low, angry voice. "I want you to leave my house right now."

Blood drained from his face. "Mr. Grant, I—"

"Leave. My. House. Right. Now."

"Not until I speak with Marilyn, sir," he said quietly.

Barry grabbed his tie, yanking it. "You are not talking to my daughter again. Leave now and bring those scheming Greeves with you. You bastards don't care a whit about fair play."

"Dad? What's going on?" Marilyn said from the hallway.

"Marilyn," Jarryd called out. "I want to explain—"

"You are not explaining anything to her, you liar," Barry growled. "You're leaving and you're never gonna see her again."

"What is going on?" Marilyn pried her father's hand from his tie.

Barry stepped back but continued to glare at him with furious hatred. "Do you really know who this bastard is, Marilyn? Do you know that he is the biggest shareholder at Greeves Minerals?"

"What?" Marilyn asked incredulously.

"He is Margaret O'Neill's son. He inherited most of her estate. *In suspicious circumstances.*"

Marilyn turned to Jarryd with questioning eyes. "What's Dad talking about, Jarryd?"

134

"None of this has anything to do with how I feel for you," he said, his gaze pleading. "I love you."

"Bullshit!" Barry said. "You're using her so Greeves Minerals will win Well of Brilliance. Either you, Elliot or Olivia must have started that rumour that we weren't serious about buying it—that we're just using it as leverage for another deal."

"That's not true!"

"Why didn't you tell Marilyn you own half of Greeves Minerals when you *knew* she was considering coming back to Grant Ace to help us win Well of Brilliance—*against your company*?"

"I…" Jarryd rubbed his face. "Please let me explain from the beginning."

"So this is all true?" Marilyn asked, the hurt in her tone apparent.

Jarryd faced her. "As you know, I was adopted. Margaret O'Neill was my birth mother. I first met her a year before she died—at her instigation. She'd requested me to keep our relationship a secret for various reasons, including not wanting to attract negative publicity for Greeves Minerals when they were in the midst of sensitive negotiations. I had no idea that she'd planned to leave the bulk of her estate to me, including all her shares at Greeves Minerals. And I didn't know that Grant Ace was also interested in Well of Brilliance until after we'd agreed to go out again."

Barry snorted. "So Margaret decided to leave you a billion-dollar inheritance a mere few months after getting to know you? Why? Especially when she didn't tell anyone about you, not even Patrick O'Neill—*her own husband*."

135

"She said in her will that her grief at the death of her son with Harold and her guilt for giving me up for adoption all those years ago were tied together and that was the catalyst for her decision," he said insistently.

"How did you know all this, Dad?" Marilyn asked.

"Patrick is downstairs. When he learned that Olivia and Elliot Greeves were coming to this party, and that you're dating this bastard, he got on a plane to warn me that these three must be up to something. Patrick is going to challenge the validity of Margaret's will because she was coerced by this idiot to leave the bulk of her estate to him."

"No!" Jarryd said, raking his fingers through his hair. "Patrick accused me of manipulating Margaret into writing me into her will, but I swear I didn't do that. I was as shocked as anyone when I found out."

"You're nothing but a scumbag, Jarryd," Barry said with hostility. "You can defend yourself all you want, but you can't continue hiding the truth." He turned to his daughter. "Someone is willing to corroborate Patrick's suspicion, Marilyn. I'm sorry, but Jarryd will soon be outed as the scheming thief that he is."

Jarryd shook his head, reaching for Marilyn.

But Marilyn stepped away from him, her eyes wide with horrified disbelief. "You knew that Patrick had invited us to appear on his show, and yet you never told me that you knew him. You've never given me any indication that you've been fighting with him regarding the inheritance left by his wife. Is this why you've been dissuading me from going on *Biz Q&A*?"

"No," he said pleadingly, his chest compressing so hard that he could hardly breathe.

"All this time you were lying to me? Hiding the real truth about who you really are? You didn't even tell me you're a *billionaire*," Marilyn said, the last word filled with sarcasm.

"Please, Marilyn, it's a long story," he said desperately, his mind whirling yet not grasping the right words to say. "Please let's sit down so I can explain everything."

Marilyn's eyes filled with angry tears. "But you never meant to explain *anything*, did you? You were still lying to me just a few minutes ago when I told you about Elliot. You pretended you didn't know him and yet you obviously do. *He's the COO of the company you half-own.* Is that why you're both so keen on dating me? To see which one I'd fall for so either one of you can screw me and use me?"

"No! Don't you say that!"

Barry put an arm around her daughter's shoulders. "Leave now, Jarryd, before I call the police."

"Marilyn," Jarryd said pleadingly. He couldn't go yet. Not until she listened to him. Not until he told her everything. Not until she understood and forgave him. Fuck, he'd stuffed up majorly, but she had to let him explain.

"Leave, Jarryd," Marilyn said, her voice cold as tears cascaded down her face.

"Please."

"At least have the decency to go before any more guests arrive. Let us continue with this party without people like you here," she said bitterly.

He sighed raggedly, Marilyn's words wounding him. Perhaps she was right. He'd done enough damage for tonight. He should go quietly to avoid Barry having to forcefully remove him from his home. That would create a bigger scandal for them.

"I'll talk to you later," he said softly, then headed for the stairs with Barry behind him. Tomorrow he'd try to talk to Marilyn again. If she refused, he'd try again the next day, and the next, and the next, until she did. He'd show her that if there was one thing he never lied about, it was that he loved her.

"Wait," Marilyn called.

His heart skipped, hope sprouting as he turned around.

Marilyn held a fisted hand towards him. "Take this."

He opened his palm and she dropped her heart lock necklace on it.

"I want my keys back."

Struggling to hold back tears, he reached into his pocket, fished out her keys, and gave them to her.

Marilyn snatched them from his hand and went to her old bedroom, shutting the door with a bang.

Jarryd had to force himself to breathe as his heart twisted in pain.

CHAPTER THIRTEEN

"Marilyn, Patrick O'Neill is here."

Marilyn hid a sigh. She didn't want to meet with Patrick, but she and her family owed the man something for what he'd done last Christmas Eve. The least she could do was to see him for ten minutes, which was all Patrick had asked.

"Give me a couple of minutes, then send him in," she told her PA, who nodded.

She leaned back in her seat and closed her eyes. Perhaps she should have followed her mother's suggestion and taken more time off work. It had only been two weeks since she'd learned that Jarryd was a heartless liar.

She was still kicking herself for not telling her friends about her and Jarryd dating again the minute it had happened. She would have found out from Natasha earlier that Gavin had done a check on Jarryd months ago.

Back then, Gavin had been hell-bent on making sure Natasha was safe from a criminal who'd become Gavin's personal enemy. Since Jarryd was a new acquaintance who'd invited Natasha to some party, Gavin had done some digging to ensure Jarryd wasn't connected to his enemy.

Jarryd wasn't in any way involved with the criminal Gavin was protecting Natasha from, but along the way, Gavin had discovered that Jarryd was very rich. Unfortunately, having been satisfied that Jarryd wasn't a suspicious character, Gavin had dropped the investigation and hadn't told anyone about Jarryd's wealth status until he'd mentioned it to Natasha during the party at Rick and Lexie's. Both Gavin and Natasha had simply assumed Jarryd didn't want to make a big fuss about his wealth, just like Marilyn avoided telling people who her parents were.

Well, didn't that show that Jarryd was a cunning con artist? He'd managed to fool not only her, but also her friends into believing he was a nice, trustworthy guy.

Would things have been different if she'd known that Jarryd was a billionaire from Natasha or Gavin instead of learning about it from Patrick and her dad?

She shook her head. What was she doing thinking about him again? She'd already spent a cheerless week between Christmas and New Year's Eve, not wishing to be part of the festivities.

At least she'd been able to get out of bed and drag herself to the office for the last three days. But she certainly wasn't getting any work done. Most of her brain power was being used to push away the constant memories that she never, ever wanted to remember. She was supposed to be working on handing over the management of her business brokering firm to one of her managers so she could free herself to work back at Grant Ace. Unfortunately, nothing was capable of distracting her from her unwanted thoughts.

Her heart compressed once again, her eyes stinging. Damn it! Why couldn't someone invent a pill for heartache? They'd be a gazillionaire!

She shook her head vigorously and took a large gulp of tepid coffee. Ugh. This was the third cup that she'd forgotten to drink before it had gotten cold on her.

A knock on her door had her standing up and putting a smile on her face. Her PA ushered Patrick in.

"Hello, Patrick," she said, walking to him and extending her hand for a shake.

"Marilyn, Happy New Year," Patrick said, giving her a kiss on both cheeks instead.

"Thank you. Happy New Year to you too. To what do I owe this visit?" she asked congenially, gesturing for him to take a seat and going back to hers.

"I just wanted to make sure you're okay," Patrick said gently. "In hindsight, I probably should have been more mindful of when and how I approached the situation. I let my own emotions get in the way and picked the wrong time to tell you and your parents what I'd suspected."

"Thank you. I'd still say you had the right timing. We were able to get rid of the Greeves and Jarryd before the rest of the guests arrived. Only my friends were there to witness the whole thing."

"Yes," Patrick said sympathetically. "I'm just grateful that Olivia and Elliot arrived ten minutes early. Did you know that they contacted me on Christmas Day to threaten that they'd make my life hell for spouting 'lies'?"

"No," she murmured, torn between curiosity and not wanting to know at this point in time.

"I said I stand by my words and that *they* should prove that I've lied about them and Jarryd colluding to beat Grant Ace in acquiring Well of Brilliance," Patrick said, the hatred in his voice apparent. "It makes me wonder if Olivia and Elliot somehow helped Jarryd in manipulating Margaret to rewrite her will."

Marilyn inhaled sharply. "How do you know for sure that Margaret was manipulated?"

Patrick frowned. "Can you really see any other reason why my wife wouldn't have told me about Jarryd? Why she never said anything about giving him the bulk of her estate? Margaret and I had a close relationship where we talked about our respective businesses and finances openly, so I'm finding it very hard to believe that she simply hadn't been ready to tell me about Jarryd. She'd kept the news about him secret for one whole year—and who knows for how much longer if she hadn't died. I'm not angry that Margaret only left me a small portion of her wealth. I might not be a billionaire, but I'm financially independent. I don't need Margaret's money. What I'm incensed about is the thought of my wife being so afraid that she wasn't even able to speak out about someone forcing her to do something against her will."

Marilyn took a long slow breath, trying to keep a lid on her own emotions. What the hell was wrong with her? Her stupid heart was still rebelling at the thought that Jarryd was a scammer. It kept on whispering to her that he simply couldn't be.

But Patrick's suspicion made more sense to her than any other reason Jarryd might have. She'd spent sleepless nights considering many possibilities, but with Jarryd having hidden the truth of who he was—and only admitting to it when he'd been caught—how could she believe anything else he had to say?

This wasn't the first time she'd been betrayed by a man. Never again. And no way she'd let the same man fool her more than once.

"I'm sorry," Patrick murmured. "You must still be hurting. But he doesn't deserve any consideration from you, Marilyn."

She smiled. "I'll be fine. Anyway, thank you very much for coming. I appreciate it."

"There's something else I want to discuss with you, if you don't mind."

Yes, she did mind. She wanted to be alone now. But she was unfailingly polite. "Sure."

"You guys haven't pulled out of the Well of Brilliance negotiations, have you?"

"No. And even though we've come to certain conclusions, we're keen to avoid accusations of defamation because we really don't have any concrete proof that Jarryd, Olivia and Elliot meant to get sensitive information from us Grants. It looks like we caught them before they were able to. But Dad did mention to Lorna Tramwell that he kicked Jarryd out of his house on Christmas Eve for lying to me. I'm sure the Tramwells can put two and two together."

"Right. Well, I want to lend my weight to your cause, if you'll let me. I hate that I'm going against the company that my wife used to lead, but I can't stand the thought of those people winning anything. So how about I promise the Tramwells a guest mentor spot on *Biz Q&A* for, say, six episodes as part of the Grant Ace bid? That will be three sessions for each sibling. They can mention the new ventures they want to go into and it would be a huge free promotional opportunity for them. As you know, there's a long line of business owners waiting for me to accept their request to go on the show. Only you Grants seem not to want a spot on it," he added teasingly.

"That's very generous of you."

"I have a personal connection to this case because of what Jarryd did to me, and I want to be on your side. You really wouldn't want a man who doesn't care about breaking your heart to win Well of Brilliance, do you?"

That heart Patrick was talking about felt a sharp pinch. "No."

"So would you accept my offer? I'm not asking for anything in return. As long as those bastards don't get what they want, that'll be payment enough for me."

She gave herself a long moment to think, but she saw no reason to say no, and every reason to say yes. "Thank you. I accept on behalf of Grant Ace. I'm sure my parents would be as appreciative about this as I am."

"Great! I'll have my secretary type up my offer and you can send it to the Tramwells." Patrick got up from his chair. "And I wish you all the best, Marilyn. It might not be my place to say this, but please don't put any more energy into thinking of someone who doesn't deserve another minute of your time."

"Thank you, Patrick."

"You're welcome."

She walked Patrick to the lifts and hurried back to her office, shutting the door before fat tears rolled down her cheeks. She angrily wiped them away. Why was she still wasting emotions over a guy who'd only meant to use her for his own gain? And what was wrong with her for attracting these types of men? Was she too trusting? Too desperate? Too dumb when it came to matters of the heart?

Well, no more. She'd rather be alone for the rest of her life than risk being used like this again.

She heard the faint vibration of her phone on her desk and her heart jumped. Hesitating for a beat, she checked who'd sent her the text.

Jarryd. Again.

Hi. Just me with another request to see you so I can explain. Please?

She deleted it. Again. Why she hadn't blocked him yet, she didn't know. Maybe she should now…

Marilyn shook her head. She might need to communicate with him later—if Grant Ace needed to take action against him, Olivia and Elliot.

She blinked back the tears that pooled in her eyes. Argh, damn him!

What she'd love right now would be to be with one of her friends. She hadn't wanted to burden them with her gloomy mood, especially during what was supposed to have been a happy time of the year, so she'd stayed away from them, only communicating via text and phone calls, and requesting that no one ask her about Jarryd.

But had any one of them contacted Jarryd, or had Jarryd tried to talk to one of them? She was so tempted to ask, but doing so felt like looking back. And she didn't want to look back. Not at anything involving Jarryd. She just wanted to keep going and focus on her goal: to heal from Jarryd's betrayal. Until she'd achieved that, she didn't want to discuss him at all. Like Patrick had said, he didn't deserve another minute—heck, another *second*—of her time.

Her phone rang in her hand and she smiled. "Hey, Simon. Great timing."

"Why?" Simon asked.

"I was thinking I need some company for lunch. Are you free?"

"Funny you say that, because that's exactly what I'm ringing you for. I'm heading to your area now and have a couple of hours free before my meeting."

"Great! Shall we meet at the café across the road from my office that make organic smoothies?"

"Sure. I'll be there in about fifteen."

"Okay, see you then."

She sat back on her chair, looking around her desk. She had a few minutes to kill before lunch.

But she didn't want to start any work. What was the point when she'd been unable to concentrate all day? Well, all week, actually. She sighed and grabbed her bag from her drawer. Might as well go to the café early and save a table while waiting for Simon.

"Going to lunch," she mouthed to her PA and exited the building. She was hit by the stifling humidity. Hurriedly, she crossed the road and entered the coffee shop, thankful for its air-conditioned comfort and relaxed ambiance. The place was already busy even though it was only eleven thirty. Everyone else must have been trying to escape the heat. Fortunately, a table had just been vacated by two women, and a server motioned for her to take it while he cleared it for her.

Smiling her thanks, she took her seat when the table was ready. She checked the menu that was propped on a holder at the edge of the table, not really feeling hungry. Then again, she hadn't been eating well. But she should order something substantial or Simon would notice her lack of appetite and make a big fuss.

"Marilyn."

Her breath hitched at the voice. What the hell was he doing here?

Reluctantly, she looked up and her lips parted in surprise.

Jarryd's eyes were sunken, as if he hadn't slept well for days. And his hair was unruly, like he'd been running his fingers through it repeatedly.

"I saw you walk in," Jarryd said. "Could I please join you?"

It took her a few seconds to find her voice. "No. I'm meeting Simon."

Jarryd's jaw seemed to clench. "Do you mind if we talk while you're waiting for him?"

She swallowed. "Why are you here?"

Jarryd's lips tugged up mirthlessly. "I was hoping to bump into you."

She stared at him, her eyes not wanting to obey her brain, which was ordering her to look away.

"Please?"

The quiet desperation in Jarryd's voice made Marilyn nod her head.

"Thank you," Jarryd said with relief, taking the seat opposite her.

"You only have five minutes. Simon's coming," she added in a flat tone.

"Okay."

She inhaled deeply. What on earth was she doing agreeing to talk to him? Sure, he seemed miserable, but for all she knew, this look was part of his plan to butter her up and get away with his abhorrent act. Or perhaps he was having sleepless nights because he knew how much trouble he was in for what he'd done.

So was she going to be stupid again? Hell, no!

"Frankly, I don't think there's anything I want to talk to you about," she said in a loud whisper that only he could hear.

Jarryd sighed. "I probably don't have much time before Simon gets here, so I'm just gonna go straight to the point. Do you really think I could have faked my feelings for you? Did it look like I was only acting all those times I made love to you? You didn't believe me before when I said we didn't have any spark—and that's because we did have a spark. More than that, we *burned* for each other. Everyone else saw that too. So how can you think I wasn't being truthful when I said I loved you?"

She snickered. "Come on, Jarryd. Love and sex don't necessarily go hand in hand, so don't give me that crap about being in love with me just because we were good in bed together. You found me attractive, but most men do. I opened my legs for you and you took what I offered. Most guys would have taken the opportunity had I made them the same offer. What we did together wasn't anything special."

Jarryd's eyes hardened. "Please don't talk like that."

"Well, I know better than to listen to a guy who was practically lying to me every single day," she said bitterly. "I don't even know who you are, Jarryd. How can you expect me to believe anything you say when the person I got to know wasn't the real you?"

"But that was me! That was all me!"

Marilyn leaned across the table, shooting him a disgusted look. "Oh, really? So who was Margaret O'Neill's son? Who's the half-owner of Greeves Minerals? Who's the billionaire? Those are the things that you kept from me. Why? Because you want a girlfriend from an influential family to help save your image when Patrick goes ahead with challenging the validity of Margaret's will? Or because you want to acquire Well of Brilliance? Or maybe it's both, huh?"

Anger flashed in Jarryd's eyes. "None of those is true."

"Unfortunately for you, Patrick is kicking up a stink," she continued in a derisive tone. "Out of the blue, you wooed me back. Around the time my parents decided to make a bid for Well of Brilliance. Convenient, huh?"

Jarryd closed his eyes for a long moment, clearly trying to rein in his emotions. "I was honouring Margaret's wish to keep my relationship with her a secret, which meant I had to keep my inheritance and my ownership of half of Greeves Minerals a secret too. If you'd let me explain everything to you from the beginning, you'll see that I never meant to use you or hurt you. Please just give me that chance."

"Give you a chance? Why didn't you take that chance on Christmas Eve when I wanted to introduce you to Elliot? No, you had plenty of chances, Jarryd. *Plenty.* But you were you still lying to me till the very end, until you got caught with your pants down. Now you're just trying to salvage the situation as much as you can. And because I told you I loved you, I bet you're hoping that I'll continue to be stupid enough to listen to more of your lies so I'll help save your ass from whatever legal action might be coming your way. No more, Jarryd. I'm done being used by you. Done."

"Marilyn," Jarryd whispered pleadingly, his eyes moistening.

Her heart lurched at Jarryd's look of despair, but she hardened it. God, he really was a great actor. A great con man. "I want you to leave me alone, or I'll be forced to hire someone to stop you from coming near me."

"Hey," Simon said, appearing by her side and touching her shoulder. "Is everything okay?"

"Yes," she answered. "Jarryd was just leaving."

She didn't look up when Jarryd stood up and left the table. But, unbidden, she stole a glance as he was exiting the premises. All she saw was his back, and that could very well be the last she'd ever see of him.

Her heart ached. To her consternation, it was not from anger, but from grief.

CHAPTER FOURTEEN

Jarryd walked out of the coffee shop, his vision blurry and his chest so tight he wondered if he was having a heart attack. But who cared if he was? If he had to be admitted to a hospital, maybe Marilyn would finally take pity on him and listen to his full explanation, right?

Or wrong.

With Marilyn's obvious anger, she might even give him the middle finger while he was on his deathbed.

But no, it didn't look like he was having a heart attack. Otherwise, he wouldn't be able to walk this fast towards…

Who the fuck knew where he was going? He didn't. The only thing clear in his mind was that he wanted to rip his heart from out of his chest so he wouldn't have to deal with all this pain.

He had absolutely no idea how to fix things with Marilyn. He could see why she now hated him so. Her assessment of the situation was totally understandable, even though she'd come to the wrong conclusions. Putting himself in her shoes, even he would think he was the worst kind of asshole.

Their mutual friends must have also come to that conclusion. He'd lost a lot of them—or so he assumed, considering that Simon hadn't even said a single word to him.

He'd texted them all after Barry had thrown him out of the Grants' mansion. He'd given them an out not to contact him, saying he'd need time to sort things out and would explain everything in due course. But he'd pleaded with them to make sure that Marilyn was okay.

He'd received their responses—mostly saying "okay." He had no idea what they thought of him after that event on Christmas Eve. He wouldn't be surprised if they all believed Patrick. Who wouldn't?

Yes, it was all his fault. No matter how much justification he had for his actions, the bottom line was he'd been too afraid to trust anyone with the truth—Marilyn, especially. It served him right to suffer like this for hurting her like he did.

But what could he do to make her understand that she was wrong in her assumptions? He might deserve Marilyn's wrath, but he couldn't stand the thought of her believing that she was nothing to him but someone he'd only used for his own gain.

He needed to find something—anything—that would somehow make Marilyn believe that he wasn't a heartless scammer before he lost all opportunity to win her back. That was, if he hadn't totally lost her already.

Jarryd stopped at the lights and glimpsed an ad for Well of Brilliance on the body of a passing bus. He frowned in thought, then turned around to walk the other way.

Twenty minutes later, panting and sweaty from the heat, he was entering the Greeves Minerals building. He didn't have an appointment to see Olivia, but damn it, he owned half of this company, right? He should have access to the CEO on short notice.

He took the lifts to the top floor and plastered a smile on his face when the doors opened. "Good afternoon, Lilah," he said to the receptionist.

"Mr. Westbourne! Good afternoon, sir," Lilah said with a smile, her brows furrowing slightly as she took in his appearance.

"Is Mrs. Greeves in? I don't have an appointment, but it's an urgent matter."

"Let me check if she's free, sir."

Lilah spoke with someone else, presumably Olivia's secretary. There was a few seconds' wait, when Lilah smiled at him shyly, before frowning at whatever the person on the line was saying to her.

"But Mr. Westbourne said it's urgent—that's why he didn't worry about making an appointment. He came straight here."

Jarryd hid his smile. This was the kind of employee he wanted working for him.

After another few seconds' wait, Lilah smiled smugly. "Mrs. Greeves is waiting for you, Mr. Westbourne."

"Thank you, Lilah. Great job," he said with a grin before heading to Olivia's office.

He still wasn't sure if he was doing the right thing coming here to talk to Olivia. But something told him this was worth pursuing.

"Hello, Jarryd," Olivia said in a bemused voice when her secretary ushered him to her big room.

"Hello, Olivia. Thanks for seeing me."

153

"I wouldn't have if it wasn't for my curiosity as to what this is about. It's urgent, you say?"

"Something like that."

Olivia stared at him questioningly as they sat down on adjacent two-seater sofas. "Have you been ill or something?"

He chuckled. "No."

"You just look…"

"Like shit. I know."

"Your words, not mine," Olivia said with a dry laugh. "Anyway, what brings you here? I've tried to contact you numerous times until that lawyer of yours told me to talk to him about anything I want to discuss with you. I have to tell you, I was insulted by that. I'm the CEO of a company who couldn't talk directly to the biggest shareholder at a time when a big scandal could be breaking."

"I'm sorry about that. Carl is just the careful type who wants to make sure that this *scandal* won't become public. But he doesn't know I'm here."

Olivia's eyebrows lifted.

"I'd like to ask you about Margaret," he said.

Olivia blinked at him. "Wow, I wasn't expecting that."

He smiled lopsidedly. "You weren't expecting me to get Margaret's shares in Greeves Minerals. *No one*, not even me, had expected that. But I assume you knew Margaret well, having been married to Harold's brother and having worked with her for years. So I was wondering if there was anything at all that she said to you to indicate that she'd been searching for me—the son she'd given up for adoption?"

"Why are you asking this all of a sudden?"

Jarryd gazed at an artwork hanging on the wall he was facing as he collected his thoughts. "My gratitude and sense of loyalty to Margaret had me keeping things from Marilyn, and now she can't stand the sight of me. It's Patrick's accusation that's giving weight to all these question marks on my integrity. If Patrick weren't calling me a scheming thief, I doubt anyone would be so quick to think I'm up to no good. I'm clutching at straws here, but I'm hoping that I can find something that would suggest—even remotely—that Margaret *did* mean to leave me her wealth so I can have something to fight Patrick with apart from my word."

He glanced at Olivia, who seemed to be scrutinising him intensely.

"It's not even the money I'm concerned about," he continued quietly. "I'd let it all go in a heartbeat if it would clear my name and, especially, show Marilyn that I never meant to use her. But I *have* to fight the allegations that I forced Margaret into anything, and I *want* to honour her wishes. Believe it or not, holding on to this inheritance is holding on to the love Margaret has shown me in that short space of time we knew each other. I'm still in shock that she died so soon after she found me, and I just can't let go of her gift that easily. But I'm losing Marilyn because of it and I don't know what to do. So I'm hoping you have something that could possibly help me counter Patrick's accusations against me."

Olivia stared at him before standing up and walking to the window. It was a long minute before she turned to face him. "I don't have anything for you right now, but I'll let you know if I remember something."

He inhaled his disappointment. "Okay. Thank you."

"By the way, I'm assuming your lawyer has told you that we are not pulling out of buying Well of Brilliance?"

He nodded. "I understand you have to do the right thing by Greeves Minerals. Besides, it would probably look suspicious if we pulled out after what happened."

"Exactly," Olivia said.

They said their goodbyes and Jarryd left the building, feeling as heavy-hearted as he had when he'd arrived. Patrick could drag this thing out for months before anything got resolved. And even if the courts declared the will valid, Patrick could say it was merely from lack of solid proof. The popular man's reputation and influence would still give weight to his conviction that Jarryd was a scoundrel—a tag that Jarryd might have to carry forever.

And he'd never be with Marilyn again.

His eyes smarted at the thought.

He trudged back in the direction of Marilyn's office, having left his car near there. Should he try pleading with her again? But the last thing he wanted was to make her angrier. She might make good on her threat to hire a bodyguard just to stop him from trying to talk to her, and that would be worse.

He turned to the street where Marilyn's building was and slowed down his pace when he saw Marilyn and Simon walking out of the café. Clearly, they'd just finished lunch. He narrowed his eyes when Simon put his arm around Marilyn's shoulders.

Fuck.

He hoped that was just a friendly gesture. As Marilyn had said, Simon was like a brother to her.

But... Simon was interested in sleeping with Marilyn, and the two had dated in the past. What if they developed deeper feelings for each other while Simon helped Marilyn through this?

Marilyn spotted him and froze.

"I'm not here to hassle you," he answered hurriedly. "I went for a walk and was going back to my car. Just so happens that the two of you just finished lunch."

Marilyn didn't respond. She simply turned her back to him and smiled at Simon, who tightened his arm around her as they crossed the road back to her office.

Jarryd stared at them, his heart being wrung dry as he forced himself to hold back the tears that pooled in his eyes.

He wanted to yell, to run after Marilyn, to fight Simon for her. And he also wanted to sit on the pavement and bury his head in his hands.

Ah, but he'd be much better off hitting something. And he knew just where to go.

He had a new project in the suburb of Kingsgrove. His company was going to get rid of the old, small house on a big site and build a modern duplex. Work wasn't supposed to start on it until next month, but he might as well start now.

He sped home to grab one tool from his garage—a sledgehammer.

*****

Jarryd swung wide and banged the sledgehammer against the wall separating two of the bedrooms in the old house. Sections of the brickwork gave way, creating a big hole.

After three weeks of knocking down walls by himself every afternoon, this was the last non-load-bearing wall that he could hammer down with his hand-held tool. He supposed he could start yanking out the floorboards next. It wouldn't give him the same satisfaction as hitting something, but it would still be a good outlet for the anger he felt at the hopelessness of his situation.

Funny how he'd never felt so low when his finances had never been so high.

A billionaire.

And he couldn't have the only thing that really mattered—Marilyn's heart.

His phone rang loudly and he trudged to the table where he'd left his personal belongings. He wouldn't pick up if it was his parents or other buddies outside of Marilyn's circle. He was getting sick of people asking him how he was doing. Or rather, he was sick of giving the same lie that he was fine.

He snorted. Marilyn was right. He *was* a liar.

An eyebrow rose in surprise when he saw the caller. "Hello, Olivia," he greeted.

"Jarryd, hi. I thought I'd let you know that the Tramwells have accepted Grant Ace's offer. We lost."

He smiled. Well of Brilliance was now Marilyn's. Good. "Thanks for letting me know, Olivia."

"It wasn't the money," Olivia continued. "Lorna Tramwell told me that we actually offered a quarter of a million dollars more. But they were swayed by the six-episode *Biz Q&A* guest panellist exposure that Grant Ace had thrown in with their bid. They think the show is the exact platform they need to promote their various new businesses."

"Really?" he asked in dismay. Damn. Patrick was entrenching himself as the Grants' friend and business partner, and he didn't like it one bit.

"Could you come to the office tomorrow morning, Jarryd? And bring Carl Peters with you, if he's available?"

"Any particular reason?"

Olivia let out a loud sigh. "It's to do with Margaret and the question you asked me the last time we met."

His heart beat faster. "Okay."

"Can you be here at eight thirty?"

"Yes."

"Good. See you tomorrow."

He hung up, and for the first time in three weeks, he was looking forward to something other than bashing down walls.

CHAPTER FIFTEEN

Marilyn watched as the respective lawyers for Grant Ace and Well of Brilliance strutted out of the Tramwells' boardroom after finalising the paperwork, leaving her and Lorna Tramwell alone.

It was a done deal. Well of Brilliance was now a subsidiary of Grant Ace and she was satisfied with this big win.

"I'm really glad to be working with you for three months, Marilyn," Lorna said. "Unless you plan to delegate the handling of the takeover to someone else."

"No, I want to be hands-on with this," she responded, smiling at the attractive middle-aged CEO of Well of Brilliance. "We're glad that it was our offer you accepted."

"Well, appearing as guest panellists on *Biz Q&A* was the clincher," Lorna said with a laugh. "It made your offer impossible to refuse."

Marilyn chuckled. "We were lucky that Patrick was willing to help us out with our bid. We owe him a lot."

"I hear you yourself will be appearing as early as next week?"

"Yes. It will be great timing for us to mention that Well of Brilliance is now under Grant Ace's wing." Frankly, she'd rather not go on *Biz Q&A* at all. She wasn't ready for any attention to be placed on her after everything that had happened. But this wasn't about her, and she was a professional.

"To be honest, I was leaning towards Grant Ace even without the *Biz Q&A* addition," Lorna said softly. "I didn't want to deal with dishonest people, but my brother insisted we focus on the numbers since the allegations against Jarryd Westbourne and the Greeves are unproven. I'm glad I was able to convince him that the rare opportunity of us each appearing on three episodes of *Biz Q&A* was worth the quarter-of-a-million-dollar difference between your bids."

"Thank you. I appreciate that. And we really must give special thanks to Patrick," she said in a too-bright tone, the mention of Jarryd's name rattling her a bit.

"Yes, you must," Lorna said teasingly. "Anyway, as you know, there's a big transaction that we're trying to close. Now that Grant Ace officially owns Well of Brilliance, I can reveal to you the person interested in four of our highest-quality loose diamonds ranging from seven to ten carats, plus ten one-carat ones. If the sale goes through, it will be the first major transaction for Well of Brilliance under its new owners."

"Great! So who's interested in them?"

Lorna told her the name of a shipping magnate based in Australia. "He's currently in Canada, but he's coming home in two weeks to finalise the purchase. He'll also be commissioning us to design two rings, a necklace and a pair of earrings using those diamonds as a wedding anniversary present for his wife. He's agreed on the final sale price of three and a half million dollars, excluding the custom design for the jewellery, which we haven't quoted on yet."

"Excellent."

"And you know what the other good thing is?"

"What?"

"The diamonds *didn't* come from a Greeves Minerals mine," Lorna said gleefully.

Marilyn forced out a genuine-sounding laugh.

*****

Marilyn dropped her handbag on the kitchen counter and grabbed a bottle of cold water from the fridge. She was glad it was Friday, the end of an exhausting week. With making sure her business brokering company was running smoothly without her at the helm, and learning the detailed ins-and-outs at Well of Brilliance, she barely had time for anything else.

That was a good thing. Being extremely busy took her mind away from her still-aching heart. Unfortunately, nothing distracted her whenever she came home to her empty house.

Tonight would be different, though. She'd be having a girls' night in with her friends—the first time they'd be together as a group since Christmas Eve—and she couldn't wait.

She still constantly wondered if any of them had been in contact with Jarryd, but she knew they wouldn't even breathe his name in front of her unless she brought the topic up herself. Maybe she'd satisfy her curiosity once and for all by asking. What harm would it do, right? She could always put an end to the conversation whenever she liked. They wouldn't mind.

Her doorbell rang and Marilyn hastened to answer it. She shrieked in excitement at seeing Jade, Lexie, Cassie, Erin and Natasha all standing there, each sporting wide grins and carrying dishes in their hands. She hugged the women—her best friends even though they weren't the buddies she'd known the longest.

"I've missed you!" she told them.

"You were the one who didn't want to see us," Natasha chided, returning her hug tightly.

"Well, I'm glad you're all here. And look at all this food! I just realised how hungry I am, although I still need to put that pre-made cannelloni in the oven. I literally just got home."

"I think we have more than enough to eat," Jade said as they all walked to the kitchen. "Don't worry about the cannelloni. We can heat it up later if we get peckish again. We should eat now before these grow cold—and before the four of us pregnant women get cranky from hunger."

"I agree," Lexie said, with Cassie and Natasha echoing her.

"I'm not pregnant, but I'm gonna get cranky too if we don't start eating soon," Erin said. "All the delicious smells were wafting in Lucas's Land Rover and my last meal was only a light salad during lunch."

"No prawn dish tonight, right?" Marilyn asked, winking at Natasha.

"Definitely not," Natasha said, shivering at the thought. "They still make me gag."

Marilyn chuckled as she took plates from the cupboard. "You all came in one car, I take it."

"Yes," Jade answered. "We didn't plan to come here together, but Lucas insisted I get Drew to take me here since Drew doesn't mind working overtime. So I offered to pick up the other girls as well since we have a driver."

"And how's Lucas? Actually, how are all your men?" Marilyn asked as they arranged their dishes on the dining table.

"They're good," came the short answers.

That intense desire to know if any of the guys had spoken to Jarryd hit Marilyn again, but she kept her mouth shut. It was too early in the night to start talking about the man she was trying so hard to forget.

The next two hours were happy ones and Marilyn wondered why she'd wanted to be left alone for so long. She'd missed this time with her buddies, and she was even missing the guys.

"Gavin's still on leave, Tash?" she asked. "Is he keeping his word not to work for all of January since he never had a break last year and worked on Christmas Day and New Year's Eve?"

"Yes," Natasha answered. "He's been good, except he told me today that he *has* to go back to work straight away for a particular case, even though there's still five days to go in January."

"Must be something really important." Gavin had had to decline to work personally on the matter her dad had asked him to look at.

"I think he's helping Carter again with a police matter. I have to talk to my brother and tell him that my fiancé is still supposed to be on leave. Or you can tell your husband off for me, Cass. He's more likely to defer to you than to his little sister."

"As if we could pry those two best friends apart when they're working on a case together," Cassie answered. "You know, I think the reason why Carter's not ready to quit the police force is because he's torn between joining Gavin's private detective agency and working for your family's electrical services firm. So he's staying put in his current job because he can't make a decision."

"What's your preference for him?" Natasha asked.

Cassie shrugged. "I want him to always be safe, and he'd be safest working for Garrett Electricals. But I know he loves being a detective, so I guess I won't mind if he does decide to join Gavin. They look after each other well."

"Did you know that Gavin and Carter saw Lucas at work earlier today?" Jade asked.

Cassie and Natasha shook their heads.

"They were going out for coffees and I wanted to join, but they didn't want me to go with them," Jade said.

"Maybe because Lucas didn't want you drinking *coffee*," Erin quipped.

"Well, I've hardly had any caffeine since I got pregnant. Luckily, I'm not craving it at all. But no, it didn't look like a strictly social outing. I did ask what they were going to talk about, but Lucas said it was a boys-only thing."

"Boys only, huh?" Lexie said. "So they keep things from us too, hey?"

Erin chuckled. "Whenever Brad asks me what we girls talk about during our girls-only get-togethers, I finish answering him in a couple of minutes. And then he'll say, 'But what else did you discuss in more than four hours?'"

Lexie snickered. "I know. Rick is just as intrigued. They must think we talk about them."

"We do!" the others said.

Marilyn laughed along, but her curiosity had been piqued and she was having difficulty ignoring it. "Hey, do you think they've talked about Jarryd? Actually, has any of you spoken with him at all?"

The laughter quickly died as the girls confirmed that they hadn't.

"What about Lucas, Jade?"

Jade shook her head. "We all got the same text from Jarryd where he asked us to give him time to work things out. He said he'd explain eventually. Lucas is a bit angry with him—we all are—so we haven't contacted him at all. We're waiting for his explanation."

Marilyn looked at her other buddies, who nodded their heads.

Then she burst into tears.

Oh, for heaven's sake! She had been doing so well! Why on earth did she have to ask about him?

"Hey," Natasha murmured beside her, rubbing her back comfortingly.

"Sorry," she said, taking a deep breath. "I didn't mean to bring him up. I was just curious."

"You can let it all out," Lexie said soothingly. "We're here."

That broke the dam that she'd thought she'd already emptied. She sobbed softly for several minutes while her friends lent her their strength by sitting quietly by her side.

When her sobbing stopped, she blew her nose on some tissues. "Sorry, I'm okay now."

"No need to be sorry," Natasha said. "You have every right to cry."

She smiled. "We should have more dessert. I have chocolate ice cream in the freezer."

"I got it," Erin said, jumping up from her seat and walking to the cupboards to get some bowls.

"I'll help scoop," Cassie said, going to the fridge and grabbing the tub of ice cream. "Just talk loudly so Erin and I can hear you from here."

She laughed. Her girlfriends were truly wonderful.

"I take it you haven't heard from Jarryd either?" Natasha said gently.

"Actually, I've been hearing from him every single day since Christmas Eve."

Everyone looked at her, their mouths hanging.

"He's been calling you?" Lexie prodded.

"At first. But I never answered, so he resorted to sending me two or three texts a day. Then he turned up at the café outside my work about three weeks ago, when I was meeting Simon. I told him exactly what I thought of him and… well… I threatened to hire a bodyguard if he approached me again. That was the last I've heard from him." And, she hated herself for it, but she felt some disappointment whenever a day had ended and there had been no communication from Jarryd.

"What were his previous texts about?" Natasha asked.

"They're mostly the same thing—pleading with me to give him the chance to explain everything. I have to say I'm surprised that he hasn't contacted any of you. I was assuming that he'd also approached you to justify himself."

Natasha shook her head. "Like the others, the only communication Gavin and I got from him since Christmas Eve was the text where he asked us to give him time to sort things out. He did plead with us to make sure you were okay, and in his text to me, he'd added that it was the only thing that mattered."

Marilyn stared at Natasha. "What's the only thing that mattered?"

"That we make sure you're okay," her friend said softly.

Tears rushed to her eyes again.

"What was he like when you saw him at the café?" Jade asked.

"Well, he looked tired… sad… miserable…" She let out another sob. "I'm so confused. Part of me wants to hear his explanation, and another part of me keeps saying that I'd be the world's biggest idiot if I entertained his request."

Cassie squeezed her shoulder, placing a big bowl of ice cream in front of her.

She took a spoonful of it, trying to clear her muddled head.

Muddled.

Hadn't Jarryd used that same word to explain why he'd broken up with her before?

She sniffed. "So did he lie to me simply because he was trying to respect his birth mother's wishes? He told me that the reason he didn't tell me about being Margaret O'Neill's son was because Margaret had wanted to keep their relationship a secret to avoid negative publicity against Greeves Minerals while sensitive negotiations were happening. He insisted he hadn't lied about his feelings for me. But how can I believe him when the case against him is so strong?"

"Let's think about this," Natasha urged. "Why exactly is the case against him strong?"

Marilyn frowned in thought. "Well, Margaret had only known him for a year and then she made a new will to leave him billions of dollars in assets."

"He *is* her son," Lexie said. "Her other son had already died, and I can understand why she felt especially close to Jarryd after that."

"Who was supposed to inherit her estate before she changed her will?" Cassie asked.

"Patrick," Marilyn answered. "Apparently, Margaret had made a previous will naming him as the beneficiary."

"Maybe Margaret changed her mind after she met Jarryd, who is her *son*," Natasha said. "And she just didn't know how to tell Patrick."

"Yeah," Lexie said. "And she'd probably thought she had plenty of time to tell Patrick about it later."

Marilyn looked at her friends, her heart beating fast. "Are you girls saying that Jarryd never meant to lie to me?"

"It's a *possibility*," Erin said. "My first reaction to what happened at your parents' on Christmas Eve was disbelief, then anger at Jarryd. How could he not tell us who he was? On the face of it, he lied to all of us, especially you. But what if Jarryd *is* telling the truth? Remember that even though Patrick is alleging that Jarryd coerced Margaret, there is no proof. What if the only mistake Jarryd made was to hide this from all of us?"

Jade nodded her head excitedly. "Lucas and I have been discussing this, because Lucas has been hurting too. We've wondered if our reaction to Patrick's serious accusations was exactly what Jarryd was afraid of—that everyone would believe Patrick and not him. What if he was keeping it a secret until he had proof that Margaret *did* want to leave him all that wealth? But how he's gonna prove that, I don't know. Margaret's gone, and she doesn't seem to have told anyone about him."

Marilyn stilled. What if Jarryd was telling the truth but just had no proof to back him up?

If that was the case, Jarryd would have been so crushed that no one believed him over Patrick, least of all the woman who'd professed love for him. "Oh, God," she whispered, burying her face in her hands.

"Hey," Jade said, giving her a sympathetic back rub. "Jarryd could be telling the truth, or Patrick could be right about him. We simply don't know at this point. None of us have known Jarryd for more than a year. Lucas is his oldest friend in our circle, but at the time they first met, Jarryd had already been reunited with Margaret. So who really knows what the truth is? But I vote for finding out what it is. Maybe we could start communicating with Jarryd, interrogate him separately, and then let's try to figure out if he's being honest or not."

"And don't forget the guys—especially Carter and Gavin," Cassie said. "Those two alone can probably crack this case open."

"But where will be the fun in that?" Erin said teasingly. "Seriously, though, if Jarryd is a scammer, he'd

170

be more than suspicious if Carter and Gavin suddenly started asking him questions. If he has something to hide, he'd be more careful answering two detectives. I say we use our women's intuition first before getting any of the guys involved."

"Good point," Cassie conceded.

Marilyn stared at her friends, hope creeping out from somewhere deep inside her. But she reluctantly pushed it back down. She'd have to wait until her girlfriends found out something more substantial regarding Jarryd's innocence before she considered exposing her heart to further hurt. Simply, she didn't think it would survive another hit if her friends decided Jarryd was a liar and a con artist.

CHAPTER SIXTEEN

Jarryd stared at the text he'd received. What a total surprise. Erin was asking how he was.

It had been more than a month since he'd had communication with any one of his and Marilyn's mutual friends. While the ball was still firmly in his court in terms of explaining what had happened, he was glad that one of them was reaching out to him. But, damn, what timing.

Sighing, he poised his thumb over the keypad, debating what he should say. Well, the question was short and sweet, so hopefully a quick answer should suffice.

Hi, Erin. I'm okay, thanks. Hope you and Brad are well.

Erin's response was swift.

I've just come out of a meeting with a client close to your office. Want to go for a quick drink?

He let out a harsh sigh. How should he handle this? Pressing his lips together, he texted back.

Sorry, I'm not in the office. I'm at a work site. Next time, maybe?

There. He'd just have to make sure he didn't go out of the office until much later. Erin might see him and discover he'd been lying. The phone vibrated in his hand.

Sure. I'll be back at my client's tomorrow and on Wednesday. Any chance then?

Argh.

Unfortunately, I won't be coming to the office at all this week. Maybe I'll let you know when?

Okay, definitely let me know. We're worried about you and want to see how you're doing.

Thanks, Erin. I appreciate that.

And he did appreciate it. Big time. Someone was finally willing to give him the benefit of the doubt regarding this debacle. It wasn't Marilyn, but would Erin have approached him like this without Marilyn's blessing? He'd like to think she was aware. That would mean she still cared a little bit, right?

He shook his head. What good could come out of endless hoping? It kept him in an emotional roller coaster that zapped him of vitality.

So no more hoping, just like no more pleading with Marilyn. It would be much better to focus his time and energy on things that were likely to give him results.

*****

Jarryd entered his office building and stopped as if he just hit a brick wall.

"Hi!" Erin said, standing up from the waiting room couch.

"Hi," he answered, dazed.

Erin smiled tentatively before walking up to him and kissing him on the cheek. "I know you said you wouldn't be in, but I took the chance since I was around already. Your receptionist said you'd be back at two thirty and didn't have any appointments booked for the rest of the day, so I thought I'd wait."

His brain scrambled for an excuse. "I did have something else on, but it got cancelled. I was going to let you know, but I have other work that I need to get done. Glad you're here, though."

"I should have called first. Do you have time for a quick drink? Or a scoop of gelato?"

He smiled. Could he really turn down a friend who was reaching out to him? "Sure. Gelato sounds nice."

They strolled to the café down the street, making small talk about Erin and Brad's upcoming wedding. The invitations hadn't gone out yet, and he wondered if he was still going to be invited. He didn't want to ask right now, though.

He'd never felt this uneasy talking to a good friend, and he wasn't looking forward to getting to the nitty-gritty. Surely Erin hadn't popped by for only a light catch-up.

They ordered their treats and sat at an available table.

"So how have you been?" Erin asked.

"Like crap," he said honestly. "I haven't exactly been having fun since Christmas Eve."

Erin let out a sigh. "You said you'd be contacting us to explain your side of the story. How come you haven't yet?"

His lips tugged up mirthlessly. "I still don't know how to prove that Patrick's allegations are untrue. There's nothing new for me to say and, frankly, I'm afraid that no one would believe my word against Patrick."

"But you've been asking Marilyn to listen to you."

His heart felt a telltale pinch. "Yes, because she thought—thinks—that I've used her. I'm desperate for her not to believe that, so I've been trying to get her to talk to me. Obviously, I'm out of luck in that regard."

"What is the truth, Jarryd?"

He looked Erin in the eye, grateful for the question and not bothering to hide his emotions. "I didn't coerce, manipulate, force or intimidate Margaret into writing a new will for my benefit. We didn't even talk about me inheriting anything from her at all."

"Why didn't you tell us who you really are? Didn't you think we'd have kept your secret if you asked us to?"

"I trust you guys. But from the very beginning, I promised Margaret I'd keep our relationship quiet until she was ready for the world to know. She was a big deal and it was her story to tell. Then a few months after she died, Patrick O'Neill started accusing me of stealing his inheritance. By that time, I just couldn't come out and say, 'Hey, I'm having a problem with the famous Patrick O'Neill of *Biz Q&A* thinking I'm a scamming thief.' Besides, Greeves Minerals was still in negotiations to buy Well of Brilliance, and I'd promised our CEO I'd stay quiet to avoid any unwanted publicity. As for Marilyn, I didn't expect to fall for her so hard and so fast. But the fact that I did made me even more afraid because I had so much more to lose. I was biding my time, but everything caught up with me."

Erin stared at him long and hard, and he didn't flinch.

"I hope you're telling me the truth, Jarryd, because I want to help you sort things out with Marilyn."

He smiled sadly. "Thank you. But I'd rather she believes what *I* say to her than what *you* say to her. I'm going to lie low for a while and concentrate on finding ways to convince Patrick he's wrong about me. Please don't worry about talking to Marilyn on my behalf. There's no point when she can't trust me. And right now, I have no means to earn back her trust."

Erin was quiet for a long moment until her eyes moistened. "I'm sorry."

"For what?"

"For implying I don't fully believe you."

His own eyes stung. "Thank you. That means a lot. But there's no need to apologise. I'd probably be more suspicious of me if I saw things from your point of view."

"So what are you gonna do? Do you have a current plan?"

He shook his head. "Nothing that's guaranteed to improve my situation. Anyway, I better head back. I do have a bit to do. I've neglected work for a few weeks and I'm now paying the price."

"We should catch up again," Erin said softly.

He stood up and gave Erin a kiss on the cheek. "Thank you for listening to me. You take care of yourself, okay?" Then he walked away.

He wasn't going to make promises he couldn't keep. He had a role to play and he wasn't going to do anything that would jeopardise what little chance of success it had. He might come out empty-handed, as it would be a complete stab in the dark, but he was going ahead with it. He couldn't see any other opportunity to get his life back on track.

*****

Jarryd frowned when the security intercom buzzed. Who'd be calling to see him at nine o'clock on a Friday night without prior notice?

Maybe he should ignore it. He most definitely wasn't in the mood to talk to anyone after watching the latest episode of *Biz Q&A*.

Marilyn had been in it, and she'd been wonderful. She'd mentioned Grant Ace now owning Well of Brilliance without sounding salesy or gimmicky, and she'd given sound, actionable and compassionate advice to the three budding entrepreneurs who'd just ventured into the jungle that was the world of business.

But obviously, fucking Patrick O'Neill had cemented his friendship with the Grants. And it was clear Marilyn had taken Patrick's side.

His heart writhed some more.

He had no idea what was keeping Patrick from challenging the will. Perhaps holding off was part of his tactic to ensure his success? Who knew what the man planned? In any case, Patrick was already winning. Jarryd was miserable.

The intercom sounded again and curiosity made him answer it.

"Hey, Jarryd. It's Tash and Cassie. We've come to say hi."

Tash and Cassie?

He raked his hair with his fingers. Why the hell were they here?

"Hey, girls. Give me a couple of minutes and I'll come down to meet you."

"Can we come up?"

"Uh, sure." He buzzed them in and stood by the open door as he waited for them to climb up two flights of stairs. They'd sounded friendly, and he bet Erin had spoken to them and had given her opinion on his situation. Had Erin spoken to Marilyn too?

Well, if she had, Marilyn had clearly not shared Erin's belief that he was innocent. Otherwise, Marilyn wouldn't have gone on *Biz Q&A*, would she? He let out a sigh.

"Hey, girls, good to see you," Jarryd said as the two appeared at the top of the stairwell.

The hugs the women gave him were warm and it made him feel somewhat better.

"Carter and Gavin are out somewhere, so we had dinner by ourselves," Natasha said as they went inside his apartment. "We thought we'd drop by because we were passing through here."

"Right. Want some coffee or tea? Or milk?" He glanced at their tummies and smiled at Cassie's slightly obvious bump. Natasha was wearing a loose top and he couldn't tell if she was showing already.

"Just water, please," Cassie said. "We've already had herbal tea with our meal. Have you had dinner?"

"Uh, yeah," he said unconvincingly, going to the kitchen as he poured water for his visitors. He hadn't eaten anything since he'd had an early lunch with a client. He had been hungry and had planned to order pizza or something, but seeing Marilyn on *Biz Q&A* had totally robbed him of all appetite.

Come to think of it, hadn't Cassie and Natasha watched the show?

178

"Hey, didn't you see Marilyn on *Biz Q&A* tonight?" he asked casually as he rejoined them in the living room.

"Yes," Cassie answered.

"Where? I thought you went out to dinner."

Both women flushed.

"We had dinner at my place," Cassie said. "Then Tash and I thought we'd go out to have dessert, but decided to drop by here instead."

"Why, thanks. It's unexpected, I have to say," Jarryd said lightly.

There was a moment of silence before Natasha spoke. "Erin told us that she saw you the other day. We thought we'd give you a chance to explain too."

He inhaled deeply, touched. "Thank you."

"So... anything else you want to say?"

He rubbed his jaw. "Apart from what I've told Erin? Not really. I'm still nowhere near coming up with anything that would counter Patrick's allegations. Is there something you particularly want to ask me?"

"Did you ever lie to Marilyn?" Cassie asked, her tone a tad challenging.

"Yes. Lies of omission, mainly, as you already know."

"I mean about your feelings for her."

"No. Never," he said quietly, meeting their gazes frankly. "In the beginning, I kept the truth from her because of my loyalty to Margaret's memory. But it didn't take long before my reason also became the fear of losing her. Obviously, I stuffed everything up because I lost her anyway, in the worst possible way."

179

He saw the look in their eyes turn from uncertainty to compassion.

"She's still very hurt," Natasha murmured.

He nodded. "That's understandable. She'd been betrayed by a guy before, so I don't blame her for reacting the way she did, considering the circumstances." But, damn, understanding her reaction didn't lessen the pain in any way.

"Give her time," Cassie said sympathetically. "When she's ready, we'll be happy to arrange for the two of you to meet."

He looked down on the floor. "Thank you, but please don't worry about it. Like I told Erin, I have nothing right now that would rebuild her trust in me, and I'd rather she doesn't think of me at all than think of me with hate and anger. Besides, it's become more complicated now that she's appearing on *Biz Q&A*. I have to respect her decision."

"What are you saying?" Natasha asked, her brows furrowing.

"I'm asking you to let her be."

"You don't want us to talk to her about you?"

Jarryd shook his head in confirmation, trying to stop his eyes from misting. He didn't know what the future held for him. If he would forever be a subject of suspicion due to Patrick's public profile, Marilyn would be better off not being connected to him. His story would be picked up by the media once it became known that he was Margaret O'Neill's son. And when it came to that, Patrick could make his life a complete hell regardless of the legal outcome of a will challenge. He might have his billions, but what good would that do if nobody trusted him? He didn't want to drag Marilyn or Grant Ace down with him if he couldn't find a way out of the hole he'd fallen into.

He missed Marilyn so damned much. But he wasn't going to put her in a position where she could be exposed to more hurt. And if he couldn't clear his name, he couldn't see how they could be together again.

CHAPTER SEVENTEEN

Marilyn glanced surreptitiously at her friends as she lowered herself into Jade's swimming pool. Lunch had come and gone, and they were now about to enjoy delicious treats prepared by the Biltons' chef for afternoon tea, but the five still hadn't brought up the topic she'd been waiting for all week: Jarryd.

They'd agreed to this mini pool party the last time they'd met for dinner at her place, with Jade offering to host. The men had also been invited, but they'd arranged a boys' get-together elsewhere to ensure that the women got to discuss freely amongst themselves.

Marilyn was grateful for the men's thoughtfulness, but she was disappointed that there had been no discussion happening among the girls yet—at least, not the important one she'd been expecting.

"I wonder what the guys are doing right now," Lexie said, sitting next to her on an underwater bench.

"They're probably still enjoying their fishing without some of us girls complaining of nausea or boredom," Jade said from a deckchair beside them.

Cassie snickered. "Carter just sent me a photo of him and Brad posing with their catches."

"Oh, really? I better check my phone," Erin said, getting out of the pool.

"You know that Gavin's never had any luck with fishing?" Natasha said. "It frustrates the hell out of him, and he'll probably be the last to want to leave because he'd still be trying to catch one when everyone else is ready to go home."

"I wonder if Simon brought a date with him," Lexie mused. "When Rick told him about today, Simon said he'd already promised to spend the day with a model who'd asked him out. But he also said he wouldn't mind going fishing with the boys. Rick said to take whoever she was with him, if she didn't mind spending the day with men."

Erin laughed. "If she knew how hunky all those men are, I'm sure she wouldn't have said no. But if she's there, I hope she knows she can only flirt with Simon."

"Or Tristan or Derek," Jade quipped. "You know Simon. If he's decided to forgo a day alone with one woman, he's not that interested in her."

Marilyn wanted to roll her eyes, having had enough of waiting for the "main event". "Hey, girls, are we ever going to talk about Jarryd? Didn't we say that some of you would try to contact him last week? Has anyone managed to do that?"

Her friends looked at each other.

"So you do want us to talk about him?" Natasha asked.

"Of course."

"Well, we were just waiting for you," Cassie said.

"Why? I thought talking about him was one of the main reasons we're having this pool party."

Erin let out a heavy sigh. "He asked us not to force you into discussing him, so we thought we'd wait until you brought him up."

"What do you mean?"

Erin swam to sit next to her. "I saw Jarryd on Wednesday and Tash and Cassie saw him last night. The three of us believe he's telling the truth."

Her heart banged rapidly in her chest, as if saying "I told you so" in an emphatic fashion.

"And it wasn't so much what he said, but how he said it," Cassie murmured.

Natasha nodded. "It was his demeanour, his expression. I know dishonest men could be excellent actors, but I'd say even those kinds of people wouldn't be able to fake emotions as quickly and as clearly as Jarryd did when we mentioned your name."

"What did he say?" Marilyn whispered.

"Apart from swearing that he didn't manipulate Margaret into writing a new will, he said that he never lied about his feelings for you."

Her eyes smarted as her heart continued its frenzied dancing.

"He also said…" Erin paused.

"What?"

"Well, he said that he didn't want my help in asking you to talk to him because he'd prefer that you believe what *he* has to say rather than what *I* have to say. He didn't think there was any point trying to get the two of you to meet because he doesn't have any proof that would rebuild your trust in him."

"He's mad at me?"

"No! He said he totally understands why you reacted like you did."

"But he doesn't want to see me or talk to me?"

"Not exactly," Natasha said. "He thinks you've taken Patrick's side, since you agreed to appear on *Biz Q&A*. He said he wants to respect your decision."

"He also said he was scared of losing you, that was why he'd kept the truth hidden for as long as he did," Cassie supplied. "But he knows he stuffed up and he doesn't blame you for hating him."

A tear fell down Marilyn's cheek. "I don't think I hate him. But I'm still angry at him. And although I'm interested in what he has to say, I'm scared to allow myself to trust him again. What if he's just a great actor? Can any of you *guarantee* that he's not an opportunistic scammer?"

"No," the three mumbled.

"But I have to say I do believe him and am prepared to help him out," Natasha said gently.

Marilyn swallowed. "My heart wants me to throw all caution to the wind and give Jarryd another chance. But my brain—or some other part of me that's scared—is pulling me back. It's telling me to wait until I know for sure that I really can trust Jarryd."

"Take your time in making your decision," Lexie said comfortingly. "We'll support whatever you decide."

She sniffed. "I don't want to be afraid, but I can't help it. If only I could have some sort of guarantee…"

Cassie reached out for her hand. "I can't guarantee that Carter and I will be together until we're both past eighty, which is my ideal scenario. What if one of us dies early? Or what if something happens and we need to question our relationship? There is no choice or action that we can take that will guarantee that the road will always be smooth and straight. Life is life. It will constantly throw things at us that we don't want or are not ready to deal with. But we have to keep adapting and maintain our focus on what's truly important. For me, the most important things in my life are Carter and this little bub growing inside me, followed very closely by my family and you guys. I'll fight tooth and nail if something comes to threaten us and our togetherness. Now, I'm not saying that Jarryd has to be your priority even if you still have feelings for him. Prioritising your career, your parents, even your peace of mind is just as valid. It's up to you to figure out what's most important to you, then follow your heart on that. Heartache is a possible consequence of any decision, but at least you won't be living in regret that you haven't given your all for what you truly want out of life. Just don't get paralysed by fear. That'll be sure to keep you in a place where bliss and joy would be extremely hard to find."

More tears trickled down Marilyn's face as she threw her arms around Cassie. "Thank you," she murmured, then hugged her other friends one by one. "I think I know what I want to do. I'll talk to Jarryd, see how that goes, and decide on my next step then."

"Good. One step at a time," Jade said with an encouraging smile.

Marilyn nodded, feeling lighter than she had for weeks. Yes, after a difficult period of going round and round in circles in her head, she'd be taking a step *forward*.

*****

Marilyn took several deep breaths, fanning herself with her hand. Gosh, she hadn't even gotten out of her air-conditioned car and she was already breaking into a sweat. What would she be like by the time she walked the few metres to Jarryd's office on this sunny, humid day?

At least she knew Jarryd was in. His car was parked in one of the private spots.

She hadn't made an appointment. She hadn't even texted to tell him she was coming. She had just driven here, banking on Jarryd keeping to his usual routine of doing paperwork every Tuesday morning in his office. Luckily, he'd stuck to it today.

What would he say when he saw her? How would he react? She hadn't planned what to say to him, except to let him know she was now willing to hear the explanation that he'd pleaded with her to listen to multiple times in the past.

With one more lung-expanding breath, she got out of her vehicle and made her way to the entrance of Jarryd's office, her heart pounding so hard it rivalled the clacking of her high heels on the pavement.

She pushed open the glass door and was surprised to see a new face behind the reception desk. Good. It would be less awkward talking to someone she didn't know than explaining herself to the previous receptionist, who she'd been quite friendly with.

"Hi," she said pleasantly. "My name is Marilyn Grant. I was wondering if I could have a few minutes with Jarryd Westbourne, please?"

The receptionist flashed her a smile. "You don't have an appointment, is that right, ma'am?"

"That's right. I only need about five minutes with him."

"I'm afraid he's not available at the moment. Are you looking to discuss an existing project or a new business? I can get someone else to help you."

"No, it's personal."

The woman behind the desk frowned. "I'm sorry, but he's not free. How about—" She pursed her lips as she consulted her computer screen. "Friday next week? Unfortunately, he's fully booked until then."

"I really need to see him today," she answered patiently. "He's in his office, right? His car is parked outside. So could you let him know I'm here, please? I won't take much of his time."

The receptionist sat back in her chair, her friendly demeanour disappearing as she folded her arms across her chest. "I'm sorry, but you'll have to come back when you have an appointment. And like I've said, the earliest I can book you in is Friday next week."

She repressed a sigh. "I hear what you're saying. I'll be sure to make an appointment next time. But for now, could you please just let him know that I'm here?"

"He doesn't want anyone bothering him at this time. And if you really know him personally, why don't you call him privately and arrange a time to see him?"

Marilyn wanted to roll her eyes, but refrained. This woman was obviously taking her job seriously. It was commendable, but very annoying. She pulled her phone from her handbag and called Jarryd.

"Marilyn," Jarryd answered, clearly surprised.

"Hi," she said, suddenly breathless. "I'm at your reception and—"

"You're where?" Jarryd interrupted.

"At your reception."

"*My* reception?"

Her lips tugged up at his tone. "Yes."

"You mean the Westbourne Constructions reception?" he asked in disbelief, sounding as breathless as she felt.

"Yes. But I was told you're not available, so—"

The words died in her throat when Jarryd appeared at the end of corridor by the side of the reception area.

"Jarryd!" his receptionist said. "I wasn't sure if you wanted me to disturb you. You said that under no circumstances should anyone bother you when it's not work-related."

"It's okay," Jarryd answered, but his eyes were focused on Marilyn.

Marilyn gulped, her heart wanting to escape from her chest to fling itself at Jarryd. For all her hurt and anger, she did miss him so.

But that ultra-cautious side of her that was scared of being hurt again kicked her crazy heart aside to take over once more. Instead of running to him and putting her arms around his neck like she wanted to do, she gave him a small smile instead. "Hi. I only want a few minutes of your time."

"Sure," Jarryd said. "Come on through."

She walked towards his office, hyperaware of him behind her.

"You want something to drink?" Jarryd asked as he closed the door.

"No, thank you." She sat in one of his visitor's chair.

Instead of taking the seat behind his desk, Jarryd took the other visitor's chair next to her, positioning it so he was facing her fully. "What can I do for you?" he asked quietly.

Her brows rose. Of all the things Jarryd could have said, that was the last she'd expected. But then again, she hadn't exactly let her guard down completely. He was probably following her lead.

She ordered herself to relax. "I spoke with the girls."

Jarryd's lips curved on one side. "Did they talk you into coming here? I asked them not to."

"Well, after speaking with them, I've decided it's just fair to listen to what you have to say."

Jarryd bowed his head and stared at the floor for a long minute. "I don't think there's anything I could add to what I've already told the girls."

She frowned.

"I appreciate you coming here, Marilyn," Jarryd said, glancing up, his eyes bleak. "But right now, there's nothing I can do to fix what was broken. We probably should talk later, because there's no point doing so today."

What? "I don't understand. I thought you'd been wanting to explain yourself to *me*."

"Yes. But there are things I need to do first so that I can... fix things."

"Wouldn't it be a start if you told me now what you've been wanting to tell me when you used to text me twice a day?"

"I don't think so."

190

"But... how are you planning to fix things, then?"

Jarryd shrugged. "Time will tell."

She gaped at him, but he wouldn't meet her gaze.

"You want me to go now?" she asked, a cold hand clutching her heart.

Jarryd nodded. "It's best if you do."

She blinked, unable to believe what was happening.

She wanted to stay and shake him and ask why he didn't want to talk to her, why he wanted her to go. But that part of her that refused to open herself up to more hurt urged her to stand up and leave.

So she did.

She closed the door behind her, somehow not wanting him to watch her trudge out of his office—numb apart from the intensifying pain in her heart and the utter confusion that accompanied it.

CHAPTER EIGHTEEN

"You're such a fucking asshole, Jarryd Westbourne," Jarryd muttered to himself when Marilyn walked out of his door.

He buried his face in his hands. Could he have handled that better? Of course, he could have, but he'd been unprepared for seeing her here in his office.

He stood up and grabbed his phone, calling up Carl Peters' number with angry frustration. "Can't we get the results quicker?" he said without preamble when Carl answered.

Carl chuckled dryly. "They only got them yesterday, Jarryd. These things take time, especially since you wanted five tested."

"I'm happy to pay extra to have the tests expedited."

Carl sighed. "I'll see what I can do. But don't get your hopes up with this first lot. It might take several goes before one turns out to be a dud—if they really are handing out duds."

Jarryd raked his hair. There was nothing he could do but wait—and stay away from Marilyn. Both were unpalatable, but protecting Marilyn from this potentially explosive scandal was his top priority.

Unfortunately for him, the longer it went without the result he hoped for, the more he had to push Marilyn away. He couldn't take the risk of her reading him and demanding to be told what was going on.

But she'd looked so crushed when he'd asked her to leave…

"Tell me again what the repercussions are if I told Marilyn about this," he said to Carl, needing to be reminded or he'd end up running after her and breaking down.

"If you tell her now, before you're even sure that you and Olivia have made the correct assumption, you'd be disrupting Marilyn's business. This shot-in-the-dark plan that you have won't work for Marilyn because, as the head of Well of Brilliance, she would be duty-bound to act swiftly and conduct a full investigation. That will be hard to keep a secret even if she tries because she won't know who else on the inside is in on it. If you are wrong, you'd have wrecked Marilyn's relationship with Lorna Tramwell and Patrick O'Neill. And depending on how those two reacted, it could get really ugly. I'm sure Patrick wouldn't have any qualms using his popular show to defend himself and berate Marilyn and Grant Ace for believing *you*—the guy who turned up out of the blue and suddenly got Margaret O'Neill to change her will. Do you see where this is going?"

"Yes," he said with a groan.

"Forcing Marilyn's hand to conduct an investigation now is a bad move. The culprits would have the chance to hide evidence of their deceit before we get something concrete against them. Remember that all we have is conjecture. The tests will tell us if we have

193

anything to back our suspicions with. So until one of the diamonds turns out to be synthetic, it would be better for Marilyn and Grant Ace if she doesn't know what you're doing."

"Argh!" Jarryd muttered under his breath.

"I know how hard these last few weeks—heck, this last year—has been for you, Jarryd. But keep the faith for a bit longer. If there's any justice in this world, you'll soon feel free to enjoy your inheritance without worrying that Patrick will continue to insinuate it was ill-gotten."

Jarryd shook his head. All he wanted was to win back Marilyn's love and trust. He hoped he could do so without being the news bearer of a mammoth problem that might sink Grant Ace if handled incorrectly.

*****

Jarryd stared at the envelope in his hand that contained the results he'd been waiting for.

He hadn't expected that the first five diamonds he'd acquired from Well of Brilliance would already include a synthetic one passed off as a natural. The fact that the first lot already included one synthetic had him worried. How many had already been sold to unsuspecting customers who saw Well of Brilliance as a trusted brand? And how many laboratory-produced stones were still in stock?

The elevator opened and he stepped into the reception of Grant Ace Holdings. Olivia had offered to accompany him to this meeting with Marilyn, but he'd declined. He wanted to be the one to explain to her. What was more, it was Valentine's Day. Professionally, that shouldn't have made a difference. But personally, it made him want to be alone with Marilyn, even if what he had to tell her today wasn't the kind of news she'd welcome at any time.

But who knew how his luck would hold today? Gavin had promised that he'd speak to their mutual friends before he went to work—with Marilyn being the first he'd call.

Marilyn might agree to go out for a meal with him now that she should already have gotten Gavin's confirmation that he wasn't the crook Patrick had painted him out to be.

Anticipating that he'd get contacted by a few of their buddies after their conversation with Gavin, he'd turned off his phone so he could focus on preparing himself for this critical meeting. After this important task was done, he'd spend the rest of the day reconnecting with his friends—Marilyn, first and foremost.

He presented himself to reception and the lady immediately escorted him to an office at the end of the corridor. His mouth dropped open at the sight of the person sitting behind a large desk.

"Hello, Jarryd," Barry Grant said, standing up but placing his hands behind his back.

Clearly, the man didn't want to shake his hand.

"Mr. Grant, good afternoon. I wasn't expecting you."

Barry smirked. "I know you made an appointment to see Marilyn, but she's out with Simon. It's Valentine's Day, you know."

He stared at Barry, his chest compressing. If Marilyn's father had meant to strike a blow to his heart, he'd succeeded.

Hadn't Gavin spoken with Marilyn already? Or Simon? Why were they out together? On *Valentine's Day*?

"So why are you here, Jarryd?" Barry asked, motioning for him to take a seat as he sat down himself. "You said it's about Well of Brilliance. I normally wouldn't entertain such a vague topic, but because it's you, I thought I better turn up even if it's just to tell you to stop bothering my daughter or you'll have me to deal with."

Jarryd put on an impassive face as he settled himself beside Barry. "I asked Olivia Greeves if she remembered Margaret O'Neill saying anything that could help me counter Patrick O'Neill's allegations against me," he said dispassionately. "At first she didn't volunteer any information, but on the day we learned that the Tramwells had accepted Grant Ace's offer instead of ours, she asked to meet with me. Margaret didn't tell her anything about wanting to connect with the son she'd relinquished for adoption, but Margaret did share with her important facts regarding Patrick O'Neill."

Barry put his hand up to halt him. "I'm assuming you're trying to salvage your reputation. If this is about Patrick, I suggest you take this up with him. It has nothing to do with me and, frankly, I'm too busy for it."

"If you listen for two more minutes," he said calmly, "you'll see how your company is affected by this."

Barry half-rolled his eyes and motioned for him to go on.

Jarryd wanted to yell at the man who still hated his guts, but he swallowed his emotions and continued his matter-of-fact delivery. "While Margaret did not specifically mention writing a new will, she did tell Olivia that she would make sure that Patrick would not get any more than ten million dollars of her wealth. That amount was in return for whatever help Patrick's *Biz Q&A* show had done for Margaret's and Greeves Minerals' profile, and for Patrick's efforts to show a happily married facade in public."

Barry sat back in his chair, arms crossed over his chest. But the curious look in his eyes betrayed him.

Good. It was time for Jarryd to drop the first bombshell. "Margaret didn't want what she herself had inherited from her first husband to go to her second husband because Patrick O'Neill has been having an affair with Lorna Tramwell."

Barry's eyes widened.

"Margaret had proof of this, and she'd shared it with Olivia. Olivia had kept this from me in the past because she wasn't sure about me. The first time she'd heard of me was when she learned I was Margaret's heir who'd inherited half the shares of the company she was leading. She didn't know then if she could *trust* me." He paused, shooting Barry a meaningful look at the word trust.

Barry frowned. "I still don't see what this has to do with Grant Ace."

Jarryd took a deep breath, his thoughts turning to Marilyn. He wished she was here so she could listen to his explanation and the assistance he was willing to give Grant Ace.

But she was with Simon. *On Valentine's Day*. Had they started going out? Had he pushed Marilyn into Simon's arms when she'd come to his office and he'd turned her away?

"Jarryd?" Barry prodded.

He shook his head mentally and pushed the envelope he had with him towards Barry. "Please open it, sir," he said quietly.

Barry squinted at the writing on the outside, staring at the logo of an independent and internationally recognised diamond-grading and certification laboratory. Then he pulled out the documents contained within. When he came to the fifth sheet, his brows rose in surprise. "Four high-quality one-carat diamonds and one very good synthetic."

"Yes," Jarryd replied. "I bought all of them from Well of Brilliance, and I was given a certificate of authenticity for each of them."

Barry looked at him in shock.

"I had the certificates checked too," he continued, indicating the papers that Barry hadn't looked at yet. "Not surprisingly, the one for the synthetic stone was a counterfeit."

"No," Barry whispered, blood draining from his face as he shuffled the rest of the documents to check them out.

Jarryd gave the older man a few moments for the news to sink in. When Barry dropped the papers to put his hands on his head, Jarryd said softly, "I'm not sure if you're aware, Mr. Grant, but it was Margaret who'd instigated the talks for Greeves Minerals to buy Well of

Brilliance a month before her death. Apparently, Well of Brilliance wasn't even for sale then."

"I wasn't aware," Barry mumbled.

"Well, when Margaret hired a PI to confirm Patrick and Lorna's affair, the PI also uncovered that the Tramwell siblings were having financial difficulties due to their other business venture together going south. Margaret saw an opportunity to exact revenge against the woman sleeping with her husband. For Margaret—and I'm sure for Patrick and Lorna as well—it was unacceptable for the affair to go public. Margaret wanted to avoid the circus that would definitely happen if the news came out. So she set out to buy the company Lorna was heading, which happened to be a great complement for Greeves Minerals' activities. She approached Lorna's brother, who was all for selling, given that he was close to personal bankruptcy. But Lorna wouldn't give in despite pleading from her brother. And Margaret wouldn't give up. When she died suddenly, Olivia resumed the negotiations after a couple of months. Olivia was mainly motivated by her loyalty to Margaret, but she also saw that Well of Brilliance would have been a great acquisition for Greeves Minerals."

"God," Barry murmured, his shock still apparent. "So Patrick knew that Margaret had found out about his affair with Lorna?"

"Yes. Apparently, Patrick had promised to end the affair at one point, but he didn't, and that had made Margaret angrier. All this explains why Patrick didn't challenge Margaret's will before probate was granted. He'd claimed he was too shocked and was in such grief that he didn't even think about it until later, but he obviously *knew* why he only got what he got. When he

199

discovered that Margaret had told no one about me, he must have seen it as a perfect opportunity to make his accusations that I'd coerced my birth mother. Pretty convenient for him. It covers up any questions about why his wife didn't leave her wealth to him. He has people's sympathy and trust while he continues to vilify me and hide his affair with Lorna."

"But what about this synthetic? Is this a one-off? Are there more? How did you know about it?"

"When Olivia visited one of our mines, she got to talking to a newly hired manager who used to work for a competitor that also produces synthetic gemstones. Apparently, a few months ago, Lorna Tramwell herself had gone in to negotiate a good price for a number of excellent-quality laboratory-produced diamonds that were impossible to identify as non-natural without the proper equipment and know-how. She bought thirty one-carat synthetics and took great pains to explain to the producer that Well of Brilliance would wholesale them to other stores that legitimately sell synthetic stones to those who can't afford a natural. Olivia became suspicious because she didn't notice any mention of Well of Brilliance wholesaling synthetics in any of the documents she'd studied about them."

"I didn't see that either," Barry said. "We've been assured they only ever source natural stones and retail them with proper certification. And, of course, we've done our due diligence, but it would have been impossible for us to uncover this without going through each and every single inventory and transaction. In other words, I doubt we would have known about this even if we went over and above what was already an exhaustive check. "

Jarryd nodded. "Olivia and I came to an assumption that Lorna had been selling those synthetics as naturals so she could get more profit from each. My concern is that while Lorna's working with Marilyn for a smooth takeover, Lorna might be cleaning up her act—and probably getting rid of the remaining synthetics by selling them off to unsuspecting customers who simply trust Well of Brilliance's certificates."

"So you decided to catch them in the act?"

"Yes. I asked Gavin Redford—who I'm sure you trust—to do a bit of digging around. He confirmed that Patrick and Lorna are still together. One of his operatives also saw both Lorna and Patrick visit one particular Well of Brilliance retail store at around midnight and they stayed inside for at least an hour. So I went to that store and bought two necklaces, a ring and a pair of earrings, all with one-carat diamonds. Then I sent the stones to the certifiers. Those are the reports that came back." He pointed his chin at the documents in front of Barry.

"Why didn't you tell us about your suspicions earlier?"

"To protect Marilyn and Grant Ace." He repeated to Barry all the reasons he and Carl had discussed.

Barry rubbed his jaw, his eyes getting suspiciously moist. After a long moment, he looked Jarryd in the eye. "I owe you a massive apology and an enormous thank-you," he said humbly.

Jarryd nodded his acceptance. "I'm happy to continue to assist however I can until this is all sorted. Needless to say, catching Lorna and Patrick would also be beneficial for me."

"Thank you. We have a big job to do. Would you be willing to attend a meeting with me, Marilyn and our lawyers to discuss our next steps? Perhaps at nine tomorrow morning?"

"Of course."

"Great. I'd also appreciate it if you'd give Olivia and Gavin a heads-up that I'll be inviting them too."

He nodded.

Barry looked at his watch. "Marilyn is due back any time now. She wants me to say a quick hi to Simon."

Ouch. After everything that had been said, Barry's words were like a dart thrown at his heart.

"Well, I better be going," he said morosely. He most certainly didn't want to be present to see Marilyn and Simon together *on Valentine's Day*. The last few weeks had been sucking him of strength, with sleep eluding him almost every night. Only his motivation to see this through had kept him going. Now that he'd said what he had to say, he didn't think he had any juice left to manage his strong jealousy. It would be better if he left.

"Jarryd—" Barry was interrupted by a knock on his door. "Yes?" he called out.

Marilyn came in and her jaw dropped when she saw Jarryd.

Jarryd swallowed and looked away, not wanting her to see his hurt. This wasn't the time.

"Marilyn," Barry interjected. "We need to talk. It's extremely important."

"Um, Simon's here—"

"Please tell Simon I can't see him today."

"Okay. I'll let him know."

Jarryd heard the door shut and let out his breath.

"Jarryd, please stay and help me update Marilyn with this situation."

He hesitated. Should he? It would be his chance to talk to Marilyn and explain himself finally.

But he was so very tired. And even though he'd fight for her till he had no strength left, he also needed to consider her feelings. Marilyn had a big shock coming with the Well of Brilliance news. Could he really make this day worse for her by putting her in an uncomfortable position when she clearly had just been on a date with Simon?

He shook his head. Considering his mental and emotional exhaustion, he'd probably just stuff it up further with her. "I'm sorry, Mr. Grant. But I have to go. Thank you for your time. I'll see you again tomorrow for our next meeting."

Barry walked to him and, to his surprise, hugged him tight. "Thank you very much," the older man said, choked.

"You're welcome, sir," he said past the lump in his throat.

Jarryd said goodbye to Barry and made his way to the lifts. His steps faltered when he spotted Marilyn standing close to Simon in the lounge area. Simon was holding both her hands and they were whispering to each other.

His heart twisted as his biggest fear materialised before his eyes.

CHAPTER NINETEEN

"I don't know why I'm so nervous. I don't remember being this scared about anything before in my life," Marilyn said, taking slow deep breaths to calm her racing heart.

"It'll be fine," Simon said, squeezing her hands again. "We'll go in there, I'll deliver my line that Jarryd's an upstanding guy since Gavin couldn't be here to assure your dad himself, then I'll leave you guys to it."

She nodded. "It's just that Jarryd didn't look happy when he saw me. He avoided my eyes. I think he hates me."

"Aw, come on. He doesn't hate you. Why would he hate you?"

"Because I appeared on *Biz Q&A*. He thinks I'm on Patrick's side, especially when the girls had already shown him *they* believed him."

"Don't be too hard on yourself. Just tell Jarryd that you were hurting and that the *Biz Q&A* appearance wasn't personal but a business promise you'd made."

She took a deep breath. "Okay, let's go. I don't know what they spoke about in there, but I think Jarryd tried to explain himself. But Dad still didn't believe him, judging by their expressions."

"If your dad continues to be stubborn, I'll help you hide your trysts with Jarryd from your parents," Simon quipped.

She smiled despite her heavy heart and reached up to hug him. "Thanks, Simon."

"Pleasure. I actually like seeing my friends head over heels. It makes me think love might be a worthwhile thing to pursue, after all."

She gasped in delight. "Really? You're gonna fall in love next and win the Captured by Love game?"

"Hey, don't get ahead of yourself."

She chuckled and took his arm to lead him to her father's office. She stopped in her tracks when she saw Jarryd inside one of the lifts, repeatedly jabbing a button on the panel.

"Jarryd!" she called out.

But Jarryd ignored her as the doors closed in front of him.

"No," she muttered, trotting back to her father's office. "Did you fight with Jarryd?" she asked with reproach.

Barry frowned. "No, I didn't fight with him. What makes you think that?"

"He looked angry when he left."

"I didn't do that, darling," Barry said softly. "You did."

"What?"

"Simon."

Marilyn's eyes filled. How stupid of her.

Barry rubbed his face. "Listen, Marilyn. There is something very serious we have to work on. Jarryd discovered that Well of Brilliance are selling synthetic stones and passing them off as naturals."

"What?" she asked in shock.

Barry gave her a brief summary of what Jarryd had told him. "I was wrong about Jarryd, darling. So very wrong."

She inhaled deeply. "When are we meeting about this with the others?"

"Tomorrow at nine."

"Okay. But right now I have to go to Jarryd, Dad."

"Go."

"I'll see you tomorrow," she said, hurrying to leave.

She ran for the lifts and pushed the call button, pressing it impatiently. She couldn't believe what her father had just said about Lorna and Patrick, but she pushed it away for now. The time for that problem was tomorrow. Right now, it was all about Jarryd.

An elevator arrived and she got on it, realising Simon was nowhere to be found. Where had he gone? But she didn't have time for Simon now either. Just Jarryd. She'd have to catch him somehow or he might not answer her calls. She couldn't blame him if he ignored her. She'd been so hurtful to him. So incredibly hurtful.

The journey to the ground floor seemed to take forever, and when the doors finally opened again, she rushed out, heading for the building exit, only to stop in her tracks for the second time in a matter of minutes.

Jarryd was standing in the foyer, listening intently to whatever Simon was telling him.

She walked to them slowly, blinking repeatedly to keep her emotions in check.

Jarryd saw her, his lips parting as their gazes locked. This time, he didn't look away, and a quiet sob escaped her throat. She bit her lip to stop herself from making a sound as tears cascaded down her cheeks.

Jarryd rushed to her and she ran to him, meeting him halfway. Then she was in his arms, held tightly by him.

"I'm so sorry," she whispered.

"Shh." Jarryd stroked her hair, kissing her temple repeatedly.

She didn't know how long they stayed like that until she heard a throat being cleared beside them.

"I'm happy to leave without saying goodbye," Simon said in a low voice, "but I thought I'd mention that Grant Ace staff are staring at you guys."

Marilyn pulled away, smiling shyly at Jarryd. "Maybe we should go somewhere private."

Jarryd nodded, dabbing her wet cheeks with his fingers before turning to Simon. "Thanks, bro," he said, giving Simon a man-hug.

"No problem. Always happy to help star-crossed lovers."

She reached out for Simon when Jarryd had let him go. "I owe you a lot. Thank you."

"No worries. I'll think of something you can repay me with," Simon teased.

"I know! I'll help you find a nice girl who's ready to settle down," she said with a grin.

Simon snorted.

"*Settle down*?" Jarryd asked in disbelief.

"Simon's ready to look for love."

Jarryd took her back in his arms. "And it's definitely not with this one, right?" he asked Simon lightly.

Simon laughed. "Don't worry, dude. Me and Marilyn? There's absolutely no spark between us."

"Thank God for that," Jarryd said, laughing as well as the three of them walked to the exit.

*****

"My place is closer. Shall we go there?" Marilyn asked as she got into Jarryd's car.

"Good idea," Jarryd said with a smile.

She reached for his hand to stop him from turning on the engine. "I'm sorry."

Jarryd faced her. "Hey, it wasn't your fault. And I still do have a lot to explain to you, regardless of how thorough Gavin has been. I want to clear everything between us."

"Okay."

Jarryd gave her a quick peck on the lips. "Do you want me to start again from the beginning or do you want me to answer specific questions you have?"

She took a deep breath. "Why didn't you tell me who you really are when we dated for the first time? Or even the second or third time? Or when we got back together?"

Jarryd smiled. "Apart from you not knowing that I was Margaret O'Neill's son who inherited her wealth, that person you got to know was the real me."

"Oh, honey, I know that now," she said beseechingly. "What I meant was, you pretended you weren't rich. Not that it matters to me one iota if you didn't have a cent to your name, but I was bending over backwards to make sure you were comfortable with what I thought was a very wide gap between our financial statuses."

"And I'm very sorry about that," Jarryd said earnestly. "But, simply, I was still not using any of the wealth I inherited from Margaret for personal use. Even now, I'm still living in my two-bedroom apartment, I haven't upgraded my car, I haven't bought anything of luxury for myself. Even the navy-blue dress I bought for you and the necklace you gave back to me were paid for from my savings. The only time I've ever used Margaret's money was when she invested five million dollars in Westbourne Constructions. I wasn't even going to use that, but our last conversation before she died was her pleading with me to accept her gift. I didn't want to take it—I said to her it was too much—but she said that I should consider it her investment in my business, and that she was going to expect a good return. She'd deposited the money directly to the Westbourne Constructions account before she flew to California and the money sat there for a month. She spoke to me on the phone, asking if I'd used it yet, and berated me for being stubborn and ungrateful. Two days later, she died. I thought that the least I could do to honour her memory was to use her money and work bloody hard to make sure Westbourne Constructions become as successful as she hoped it to be."

Marilyn blinked back the tears that were roused by the pooling in Jarryd's eyes.

"Then I discovered she'd also left me the bulk of her estate," Jarryd continued, clearing his throat to ward away his own emotions. "I knew that people were more inclined to believe Patrick's unproven accusations simply because of who he is. I feared then that he had the capacity to forever taint my name and make people question my honesty. Anyway, that's part of the reason why I was reluctant to use my inheritance. It was my only way to show everyone that Patrick was wrong about me. But I did use some of the cash recently—to buy those diamonds that I sent for testing."

"Thank you for that," she said, her voice hoarse. "Dad told me a little bit about it. He's very sorry for disbelieving you too."

Jarryd took both her hands and kissed them. "And I'll work with you guys until this is all sorted. I don't want anyone questioning *your* integrity and professionalism."

Marilyn melted. How could she not, when Jarryd's feelings were written all over his face? But there was something she was dying to hear.

"Do you still love me?" she whispered.

"God, yes!" Jarryd said, cupping her face. "I love you so much. Don't tell me you're still doubting that."

She shook her head, smiling. "No. I just wanted to hear it."

"And do you still love me?" Jarryd asked softly.

"Yes. I love you with all my heart."

CHAPTER TWENTY

Six months later…

Marilyn padded out of the en suite, having just finished taking a shower. She crossed the large bedroom, smiling wistfully at the sight of the king-sized bed before glancing out the large bay window overlooking Sydney Harbour. Only a couple of wispy clouds broke the blue that was the sky on a beautiful winter's day.

The brightness outside reflected her general mood. She and Jarryd hadn't been in any news for the last three or four days. The media attention they'd been getting in the last three months had started to subside.

Thank goodness for that. She'd be sure to rehire the PR company that had helped them start off on the right foot. That PR firm had arranged for a joint press conference held by Greeves Minerals and Grant Ace where she and Jarryd, her parents, and Olivia and Elliot had explained to the media the results of the police investigation against Lorna Tramwell and Patrick O'Neill. While there was still some interest in what had happened, it was nowhere near as intense as it had been when the scandalous news broke out that Lorna had been committing fraud with Patrick's knowledge and encouragement. Fortunately, *Biz Q&A* would continue on, with a different host and head panellist at the helm.

Customers were also happy that Grant Ace had replaced the twenty-six synthetic stones already sold off with independently certified natural ones despite the sales occurring prior to Grant Ace taking over Well of Brilliance. Even though they'd be losing money on that decision, Marilyn knew that showing the public they were doing the right thing was better for the company in the long run. Plus, she'd instigated legal action against Lorna and Patrick to recoup some of the losses.

And even though she'd rather not be in the spotlight, there was some news that she particularly enjoyed reading about—the goodwill from the public upon hearing that Marilyn Grant of Grant Ace was in a relationship with Jarryd Westbourne, the previously unknown son and heir to the fortune of Margaret O'Neill. Sure, there were also detractors and haters, but she chose not to worry about them.

With a contented sigh, she continued to her big dressing room and looked around, curling her toes to feel the plush carpet. She liked this setup better, with Jarryd's clothing neatly hung and folded on one half of the generous space. She had more clothes than what was before her, with her evening gowns, less-used dresses and most of her shoes kept in the other dressing room that used to be Jarryd's.

They'd both hated having to shout just to have a conversation whenever they got dressed together, so they decided that having separate walk-in closets wasn't the ideal situation they'd thought it would be when they'd bought this beautiful house together two months ago.

She'd enjoyed reorganising their wardrobe even though it took one whole day to finish a task that should only have taken a few hours. Jarryd had kept on distracting her, seducing her whenever she got a section done.

And she'd ended up having an orgasm every time.

She inhaled deeply, desire blossoming in her belly from her hot memories. Argh, if only Jarryd were home, but he'd been away for three days now to visit a Greeves Minerals mine and a gemstone-processing facility in Western Australia. Jarryd was still more than happy for Olivia and Elliot to run the company so he could focus on Westbourne Constructions, but he'd taken a keen interest in learning more about the ins and outs of the corporation he half-owned.

Fortunately, he was due back today, but not until three this afternoon. That meant that he'd be missing a chunk of Erin's birthday party starting at noon. And they wouldn't be able to make love until they got back home tonight.

Pouting, she pulled out a maroon turtleneck sweater and a pair of skinny black jeans to wear with ankle-high boots. She laid them down on the long dressing bench in the middle of the room and walked to the drawers where she kept her underwear. She tapped her fingers on her lips, trying to decide what to put on. Should she wear the matching bra and panties she'd bought from Victoria's Secret yesterday or the lace teddy that Jarryd loved stripping off her?

"How about wearing nothing underneath?" said a sexy voice from the threshold.

She turned around with a gasp before hastening to the man she missed like crazy.

213

Jarryd caught her in his arms, lifting her off the floor.

"You're back early," Marilyn said gleefully.

"Yeah. I almost forgot that I can afford to change my schedule at a whim. I finished early at the facility, so I rang Simon and asked if I could be picked up earlier than planned. Lucky he had a plane available immediately. It was a bigger one, but I thought what the heck, I'm missing my honey and I need to get home as soon as possible."

She giggled. "You can afford to buy a jet."

"What's the point when we have a friend who runs a private jet service? Isn't that why no one else we know owns a plane? Because every one of us is Simon's satisfied client?"

"That's right. Anyway, I'm glad you're home," she said sultrily, caressing his nape.

"I'm glad I'm home too," Jarryd murmured, kissing her passionately. "Especially when I'm lovingly greeted by a sexy naked woman."

"A sexy naked woman who was having horny thoughts of you," she said against his lips.

Jarryd let out a low moan, cupping her butt to press her harder against him. "What kind of horny thoughts?"

She wrapped her legs around him. "This kind, except that you should be naked too."

Jarryd walked them to the dressing bench and sat her there. Then he stood up and started unbuttoning his shirt, his gaze on her hot and wanting.

She licked her lips, leaning back to prop her elbows on the bench. She playfully opened and closed her legs as she watched him strip.

Jarryd impatiently got out of his trousers and briefs and leaned down on her, kissing her hungrily on the lips. "Naughty girl. You know what that does to me. I missed you and your pussy so much I couldn't wait to get home."

"Just my pussy?" she said with fake indignation.

He kissed her neck. "I said *you* and your pussy."

"So my pussy gets a special mention, huh?"

Jarryd licked a nipple, making her arch her back towards him.

"Of course it gets a special mention. It's my dick's favourite place."

She giggled, which turned into a moan when Jarryd touched his dick's favourite place.

"I love that you're so wet for me already," Jarryd murmured, continuing to flick his tongue on her pebbled nipples as his fingers probed her entrance.

"I really missed you," she said, gasping when Jarryd rubbed her clit. She groped down his body, finding his erection already thick and hard.

Expertly, knowing what the other liked, they took each other to heights of passion only reached by the two of them together.

Soon she was near the crest, ready to explode as Jarryd inserted a finger in her while he continued to suck and lave her rosy peaks.

"I'm so close, honey. I want you inside me," she pleaded.

Jarryd groaned, as if he didn't want to obey her but was unable to stop himself from doing so. He positioned himself on top of her. "You're not wanting a quickie so we can leave for Erin's party, are you?"

"What? No. I really want you."

"Good," he said, inserting his hardness into her. "Because I was imagining a long, slow lovemaking session for my homecoming. We'll do that after this round."

She moaned as Jarryd started moving inside her. They'd be late for lunch if they had a second round. But then again, Erin expected Jarryd to be late anyway. Erin wouldn't mind if she arrived late with her boyfriend, would she?

And frankly, Marilyn didn't care much for anything else but this moment—she and Jarryd lost in each other, joined together in the most intimate of ways, real and raw, giving and receiving with both vulnerability and power, honest in their need for an indescribable ecstasy that could only be fulfilled by the other.

"Jarryd… I love you…" she panted, almost there.

"I love you too, baby," Jarryd responded, his breathing laboured as he continued to drive into her.

And she came hard, her body bucking off the bench as she cried out her release.

"Fuck, I love you," Jarryd said with a groan, pounding into her harder, faster, then tensing before shooting hot jets of come inside her.

*****

"Hi, sorry we're a little late," Marilyn said to Erin as she gave her friend a hug.

"My fault," Jarryd said with a grin.

"No worries," Erin said with a wink. "I know what it's like when Brad and I are apart for more than two days. Anyway, Jade and Lucas aren't here yet. Apparently,

Julian had been fussing all night and had gone to sleep just before they were due to leave. They're waiting for him to wake up before coming here."

"Ooh, can't wait to see little Julian again," Marilyn said. "What about our two little princesses? Are they here already?"

"Yup, they're here. They're asleep in their portable bassinets in our guest room and Lexie and Cassie have the baby monitors in a pouch slung around their necks," Erin said with a chuckle.

"Can't wait to give them a cuddle when they wake up," she said longingly.

They walked into the large open-plan informal living area of Erin and Brad's house and greeted their other friends and the couple's relatives congregated there.

"Hey, Tash, how are you feeling?" Marilyn asked as she hugged Natasha. "No sign of the baby coming out yet?"

"No. I do hope he comes out tomorrow as scheduled. I'm really ready to see him now."

"I hope he comes out tonight," Erin said. "Then he'll have the same birthday as Auntie Erin."

"Well, I do want to enjoy this party first," Natasha said with a chuckle.

"Aha, here are the latecomers," Simon called out. "What's your excuse? You don't have kids yet."

"We were trying to make one," Jarryd quipped.

Marilyn blushed, giving Jarryd a frown.

"Oh, really?" Simon said with exaggerated surprise. "That's wonderful, you two. More babies for the group."

"He's joking, Simon," Marilyn said. "He just came back from WA, that's why we're late."

"But we thought you'd get here first before Jarryd."

She rolled her eyes. Sometimes Simon could be annoying with his teasing.

Jarryd put an arm around her waist. "So, Simon," he said. "Any news on the love front? It's been six months since you said you were ready for it."

Marilyn chuckled, pressing closer to Jarryd. How sweet of him to deflect the attention away from them and to Simon.

"Did I hear the word love connected to Simon?" Tristan asked, his eyes round.

"Yes," Marilyn said to her cousin. "Like you and Derek, he's looking for true love."

Tristan snorted. "Who said I'm looking?"

"And Derek's already found true love," Rick said.

"Hey, I haven't said anything of the kind," Derek retorted.

"I thought you're being serious with your current girlfriend, bro," Rick said.

"Nah. Why do you think I haven't got her to meet you guys?"

"But you've been going out with her for a year, haven't you?" Marilyn asked.

"On and off. And it's more off than on," Derek said, looking unconcerned.

"Anyway," Tristan said, "getting back to you, Simon. So you're now looking for love, huh?"

Simon smirked. "Not actively. I doubt I'll find it easily, though."

"Why?" Marilyn asked.

"Well, in the last six months, I dated seven women. None of them made me feel anything here the way you people in love describe," Simon said, tapping his chest.

"Seven women in six months!" Cassie said. "Maybe you need to give your feelings some time to develop before giving up too quickly. You must have been interested enough to have asked them out, right?"

"No. They asked me out."

"All seven girls?"

"Yeah."

"When was the last time *you* asked someone out?" Lexie asked.

Simon reddened.

"Whoa, whoa," Rick said. "Simon Alexander blushing. This is new. Pray tell."

"It's the sun," Simon said dryly.

"We're indoors. Come on, what's going on?"

Simon sighed. "Okay, fine. I asked three women out in the last six months. And they all turned me down."

The room went silent.

"All *three* women you asked turned you down?" Carter asked in disbelief.

"Yes. So I had no choice but to go out with the seven who asked me out."

"Oh, poor you," Lexie said with a laugh. "Any idea why the three didn't want to go out with you?"

"Yes. I think they were intimidated by the more aggressive ones who throw themselves at me. And they probably think I just want to fly them in one of my planes and induct them in my personal mile-high club."

"Well, that *is* your reputation, dude," Tristan said. "A reputation you didn't mind having, I must say."

"True," Simon said. "But I've started to realise that I'm getting sick of much of the same. It might be with different girls, but the ones I go out with are only interested in my lifestyle and the mile-high experience with me."

"You're starting to feel empty, aren't you?" Marilyn said gently. "It's not doing it for you anymore?"

"I just want to know how to not get turned down again by a girl I want to date. I don't have anything against the ones who ask me out. They're fun and lively. But I just want something like… this." Simon swept his arm in front of the girls.

"Hey, too late for that," Jarryd said, pulling Marilyn to him.

Simon snickered. "Don't worry, dude. Still no spark. But do you know what I mean? I'm surrounded by female friends who are nice, lovely girls, but I end up with, what? The players, the immature ones, the gold-diggers."

"Um, it's called karma," Derek said, "except for the gold-digger thing."

Simon's eyes rounded. "Shit. You're right."

Tristan laughed. "And he only just realised it."

"Look who's talking," Marilyn said with an eye-roll.

"The problem with Simon is," Derek said, "he's cultivated his reputation so well that most nice ladies won't touch him with a bargepole."

220

"Gee, thanks," Simon said dryly. "I already know I'm not known to be boyfriend material. Question is, how do I change that image?"

"Wow," Tristan said. "I really can't believe this is coming out of your mouth, dude."

"I just want to go out with girls who aren't all over me just because of my airplanes, muscles and pretty face. I'm starting to feel that I'm really just a plaything, that without those, I wouldn't have all this attention. Sometimes I wonder if things would be different if women didn't know who I was. Like Jarryd, when no one knew he was a billionaire. I know he snagged Marilyn, who's rich, but that's not the point. I know of women—decent, nice, beautiful ladies—who were interested in Jarryd because he's just a nice guy, not because he's a billionaire."

"Who were they?" Marilyn asked with a frown.

Simon grinned. "Ask your boyfriend. He knows who they were."

She looked at Jarryd.

"I wasn't interested in them at all, babe," he said. "It's always been only you."

She beamed at him.

"See?" Simon said, gesturing at her and Jarryd. "What's that?"

"It's love," Cassie said with a giggle.

"You know, Simon," Gavin said, "I think that if you want to break the cycle, you need to meet girls who don't know you as the rich playboy who owns many jets."

Simon nodded, deep in thought. "I have been considering that ever since I found out that Jarryd was able to hide his billionaire status. Wouldn't it be a fun experiment if I pretended that I was just a worker in my company? Maybe I'll go fly one of my planes as a pilot and work the regional route for a few weeks. See if I meet some nice girls there. My reputation is only well-known in Sydney anyway."

"Simon," Marilyn said with warning. "You can't expect to develop a strong relationship with a woman if you're going to keep from her important things about you."

"Then why are you still with Jarryd?" Simon said with an arched eyebrow.

She sighed. He had a point.

Simon clapped his hands once, then rubbed them together. "It's all settled! I'm looking forward to this experiment. We can stop talking about me now."

The doorbell rang.

"You do have perfect timing," Erin said to Simon, jumping up to answer the door.

Marilyn followed her, keen to see Jade and Lucas, but most of all their four-month-old son, Julian.

"Feeling clucky, are you?" Erin teased.

"Kind of," she admitted. "But it's definitely not yet time for babies for me. What about you and Brad? You said you'd be trying for a bub after your wedding. It's now almost five months since you got married."

"Well, we said we'll try after our big holiday overseas this year. Or *while* we're on our big holiday," Erin said with a giggle.

They greeted the Renner-Biltons and Marilyn carried Julian back to the party. The adorable little guy was wide awake, his eyes round as he took in all the people who were saying hello to him.

Marilyn sighed. She definitely wanted a little one like this with Jarryd. Sometime in the future, hopefully.

"Jade!" Jarryd said. "I've been waiting for you."

"I'm so sorry we're late," Jade said. "I'm here now."

Marilyn raised her eyebrows at the exchange. That was strange. Why was Jarryd waiting for Jade specifically? And Jade seemed to know Jarryd was waiting for her.

Jade went to the centre of the room and got everyone's attention. "Okay, peeps. You all know what you have to do. Give me the money," she said theatrically.

"For what?" Marilyn asked.

But everyone ignored her. They all reached into their wallets to hand Jade wads of cash—some appearing to be many hundreds, even thousands.

"Hey, what's going on?" Marilyn asked. She now felt as bewildered as Julian had looked moments ago.

"Hello, little kiddo," Natasha cooed, taking the baby from her.

"What's this about, Tash?" she asked, relinquishing Jade's child to her friend.

"You need to give Jade some money."

"For what?"

Natasha ignored her question, walking away as she tried to elicit a smile out of Julian.

Marilyn was about to call out her frustration when Jade clapped her hands.

"Thank you, everyone," Jade said, putting all the money in an envelope. "My charity thanks you all very much for your generous donations."

"You mean our generous *bets*, Jade," Jarryd said, turning up by Marilyn's side.

"Oh, yes," Jade said, grinning widely.

Marilyn's breath hitched, realising what was happening. When Jarryd bent on one knee in front of her, she blinked back the tears to see him clearly.

"Marilyn, you are the most wonderful, smart, beautiful, generous, loving person I've ever met," Jarryd said, his voice cracking. "I don't know what I've done to deserve you, but I promise that I'll spend the rest of my life making myself worthy of your love. You mean more to me than anything else in this world. You're my happiness, my home, my now and my forever. Marilyn Grant, will you marry me?"

She swallowed her sob. "Yes," she said as clearly as she could with her throat all closed up.

Jarryd kissed her hand before reaching into his pocket and producing a ring.

Her jaw dropped to the floor. It was a huge blue diamond, round cut, with smaller clear stones surrounding it. The band of the ring also had small diamonds set all around it. My, it was absolutely gorgeous.

"These diamonds, including the blue one, are from our WA mine," Jarryd said, placing the ring on her finger. "And I asked the best jeweller at Well of Brilliance to set them into a very special ring."

"Thank you," she said, finding her voice.

Jarryd stood up and she threw her arms around him, kissing him thoroughly as cheering went up all around them.

When they parted, their friends flocked to congratulate them.

"Gosh, it's gorgeous," Jade said, checking out her ring.

"Thank you," she said shyly. "Hey, I need to hand you money too, since you won our game."

"Yes," Jade said with a laugh. "We thought we'd give you a break with the collection for this round since it's you who captured Jarryd's heart."

"And we better start the next round before I forget," she said with a grin before calling out, "Hey, everyone, you know the drill. You have to give me your bets for the next Captured by Love game before you go home today."

"Who's the frontrunner?" Lucas asked.

"Simon," Lexie answered teasingly. "He has a plan to entice nice, wife-material ladies to go out with him. He's going to hold off telling them he's rich."

"Really, now?"

"I'm not looking for a wife," Simon said. "Just a girlfriend who's attracted to *me* first and foremost before knowing about what I can give them as a lifestyle."

Lucas laughed. "Do you even know what it's like to be on a budget, Simon? It will be impossible for you to keep your financial status from the women you want to woo."

"What's so impossible about it?"

"It's one thing saying you're not rich, and another thing to be *living* it. Just take your wardrobe, for example. You only own expensive brands that average people can't afford."

Simon pursed his lips. "Then I'll buy a whole new wardrobe from K-Mart or Costco."

"I bet you won't be able to keep it up," Lucas said.

"Hey, you wanna bet on it?" Simon asked.

"Sure."

As Simon and Lucas shook hands, Marilyn shook her head. "I was going to bet again on Simon," she said to Jarryd, "but I think I've changed my mind. I think he'll run for the hills the moment he's with a girl who asks for a long-term relationship."

"So who do you want to put your money on?" Jarryd asked, wrapping his arms around her.

"Tristan, I think."

"Tristan, my future cousin-in-law," Jarryd said with a grin.

"I can't believe I'm getting married to you," Marilyn said, resting her head on his shoulder.

"Why not?"

"Because it's a dream come true."

Jarryd cupped her face. "It's *my* dream come true."

Marilyn sighed with contentment as Jarryd placed his lips on hers. She knew that she and Jarryd would make more dreams together—and make each of them come true.

###

Thank you so much for reading!

The next book in this series, *The Unmasked CEO,* is about Simon Alexander and the woman who finally tames this playboy. To find out how Simon hides his true identity in his quest to "not get turned down again" by someone he wants to date, and how he ends up being captured by love, please visit:

http://mirandapcharles.com/books-by-miranda/the-unmasked-ceo-captured-by-love-book-7/.

CONNECT WITH MIRANDA

Be the first to know about Miranda's new releases and updates:
Subscribe to her newsletter:
http://mirandapcharles.com/subscribe/

Connect with her via social media:
Like and message her from her Facebook page:
facebook.com/MirandaPCharles
Or follow and send her a tweet on Twitter:
twitter.com/MirandaPCharles
Or follow her on Instagram:
instagram.com/mirandapcharles_romanceauthor/

Review Request from Miranda:
I hope you enjoyed this book. Please consider leaving a review, short or long, on the site from which you got your copy. Reviews from readers help books get discovered by others :).
Thank you,
Miranda xxx

MIRANDA'S OTHER BOOKS

All these books are strong stand-alone novels. But if you would like to read them in Miranda's preferred order, start with *Will To Love (Lifestyle by Design Book 1)* and follow the order below.

Lifestyle by Design Series

Book 1: Will To Love

Clarise Carson is desperate to keep her newly-engaged sister from playing matchmaker at her very own engagement party. She can't think of anything more embarrassing than have her sister's guests see her as the loser in love who can't find The One, so she drags a handsome friend to be her pretend date for the night.

Will Matthews attends his friend's engagement party purely for business reasons. He has no desire whatsoever to be introduced to single females who are after a boyfriend. He is far too focused on building his business to the success he dreams.

When Will and Clarise meet, sparks fly. Can Clarise stop her old wounds from opening up again and take another chance on love? And how can Will learn to embrace the one thing he doesn't even know he wants?

Book 2: Heart Robber

Jessa Allen knows she's plain and average, even when her well-meaning friends encourage her to believe otherwise. So when hunky and gorgeous Rob Granger asks her out, she is shocked. A seriously handsome man wants her, and that isn't something that happens everyday.

Rob Granger is a self-confessed playboy who has absolutely no plans to be tied down by any woman. He values his freedom first and foremost, and his expanding business is the only thing he is committed to. But he is intent on satisfying his intense desire for Jessa Allen who attracts him like a moth to a flame.

When Jessa agrees to a fling with Rob she finds herself falling for the man who cannot promise her tomorrow. Can she trust herself not to fall apart when the time comes to let Rob go? And can Rob ever find freedom in what he considers a prison to be avoided at all cost?

Book 3: Ray of Love

Faye Summers decides that casual dating is the way to go to ensure she's fully healed from her last breakup. When Ray Thackery, her best friends' boss, asks her out, she agrees--but only if they keep it quiet. She doesn't want the complications that may arise with her best friends' working relationship with Ray if their fling ends up in a sour note.

Ray Thackery has kept his feelings for Faye hidden for so long. Now that she is single again, he is determined not to miss this chance to make her fall for him. He's not interested in a casual-only affair. Not with Faye. He wants more than that with her.

Their relationship, beautiful and passionate when it started, quickly arrives at the crossroads. How can it survive when the two people involved have very different intentions?

Secret Dreams Series

Book 1: Secret Words

When Jasmine Allen meets Kane Summers in the unlikeliest of places, she isn't expecting the swift and immediate attraction she feels for him. But Jasmine has a secret she isn't at all comfortable sharing with anyone, least of all, the hunky guy who is literally sweeping her off her feet.

Kane Summers is a sucker for damsels in distress. When he finds himself wanting to protect Jasmine Allen in more ways than one, the instant chemistry they have for each other hits him squarely in the chest. But Kane's life is complicated, and he isn't totally free to act on the fascination he feels for her.

Kane and Jasmine are fighting a losing battle to stay away from each other. But circumstances—and certain people—beyond their control are very much intent on keeping them apart. How can they find their way past secrets and malicious intents to nurture a love that, if given the chance, could last a lifetime?

Book 2: Secret Designs

When Ari Mitchell has an unexpected one-night stand with her best friend's future brother-in-law, she fully intends to move on from it without any dramas. But Dylan Summers is someone she can't stop thinking about—— and wanting again. Problem is, he doesn't do relationships.

Dylan Summers only allows himself one-night stands for reasons only he and his two best friends know about. But after his night with Ari Mitchell, he admits to himself he has to be with her again, even if it means making things very complicated.

Their mutual attraction is simply too strong to ignore. But how can Ari find a future with a man who avoids commitment? And how can Dylan open up to the woman who can heal his heart, when he fears her true motives for being with him?

Book 3: Secret Moves

For Kristen McCann, her best friend's wedding brings out desires she can't ignore. No, it's not a boyfriend she's after--her needs are too immediate for that. After a year of recovering from a disastrous relationship, all she craves is a good, hot, short fling.

When Trey Andrews learns that the beautiful bridesmaid at his friend's wedding considered him, then scratched him out, as a possible one-night stand, he just has to change her mind. As a dyed-in-the-wool bachelor, someone as attractive and fun-intentioned as Kris is perfect for him.

But Kris has a bad habit of falling for playboys, and Trey's past is enough to put him off relationships forever. How can they grab the chance at a liberating future when painful experiences and memories of betrayal stand in their path?

Book 4: Secret Tastes

Samantha Lane wants to resign from her father's accounting practice and move to another state to follow her dream of establishing a catering business. But she doesn't want to break her parents' hearts. When her cousin jokingly suggests to tell them that a man is the reason behind her decision, she finds the perfect excuse to give her hopeless romantic folks.

Adam Craig doesn't mind playing the role of Sam's fake boyfriend. She's a friend in need and he's a helpful guy. Besides, he is desperate to show a clingy ex that they are truly over, and Sam acting as his girlfriend is the perfect solution.

When their pretense becomes all too real, a spanner in the works puts their future together in jeopardy. How can Sam trust Adam when she has proof he isn't ready to move on? And how can Adam convince Sam of his feelings when she is intent on moving away from him?

Time for Love Series

Book 1: Forever

Rebecca Andrews knows she is lucky to be hired as a private nurse for an elderly lady who is going on a one-month trip aboard a luxury cruise ship. But there's one big problem. The client is the grandmother of her ex-boyfriend—the guy she is still in love with, but who doesn't love her back.

Zach Carmichael can't say no to his grandmother's plea to join her on a month-long cruise for her eightieth birthday. But he doesn't expect his sprightly gran to bring two private nurses with her. One of them happens to be the woman who broke his heart—the one he believes lied to him about her feelings.

Aboard a luxury liner, their passion for each other flares again. Is it just a temporary flame brought about by the romance of being on a cruise? How can they give love another chance when they're both afraid to put their hearts back on the line?

Book 2: Finally

A pact with her best friends has Sarah Daley promising to make time for love after a long period of retreating from relationships. But before she embarks on finding her happily-ever-after, she wants to do something she's never done before—experience a short, hot fling. And the hunky Jeffrey Carmichael, grandson of the elderly lady who hired her as a private nurse, is the only guy who attracts her for that purpose.

Jeffrey Carmichael has long discovered that flings, not commitment, are what works best for him. After being dumped by an ex-fiancée shortly after the most devastating period of his life, he's decided that serious commitment isn't all it's cracked up to be. So when he is presented with an opportunity to start a casual relationship with his grandmother's fun and pretty nurse, he simply can't resist.

When love enters uninvited, can they admit to wanting something more than temporary? And when Jeff can't avoid welcoming his ex-fiancée back into his life, can Sarah push aside her ghosts of the past and learn to trust again?

Book 3: Again

After being dumped for glamorous women by past boyfriends, Amanda Payne is convinced she just doesn't have 'it'. So when she stumbles upon a hunky Connor Reid at a party she is forced to crash, she is more surprised than anyone when he ends up in her hotel room that night. But that fantastic experience turns into a hurtful situation the very next day.

After years of travelling for his job, Connor Reid is staying put in one place to start his own business, and hopefully find a special someone. When women he's never met before crash his work farewell party, a quiet Amanda stands out for him. But Amanda's actions the day after indicates she might not be different from her player friends.

When their paths cross again, not only are they surprised to discover that they have mutual friends, but that they also live in the same beachside suburb. Equally shocking is the fact that their attraction for each other is still unbelievably strong. But do they have a future together when Amanda thinks Connor is just playing a game? And could Connor convince Amanda that he is not the kind of man she thinks he is?

Book 4: Always

For Brenna Ward, fulfilling the New Year's resolution she made with her best friends to make time for love this year is proving difficult. The problem isn't finding a date, it's the falling in love bit... until she discovers that her best friend's brother has feelings for her.

Ash Payne has tried for years to make Brenna notice him—to no avail. Now that Brenna's dating another new guy, he's finally forced himself to accept that she'll never feel the same way about him. So he takes steps to ensure that he moves on from her—for real, this time.

When Brenna sneaks her way into Ash's every day life by working in his clinic as a part-time receptionist, the chance to explore what they could have together presents itself. But with complications from a past relationship muddying the waters, can Brenna convince Ash that her intentions go beyond merely feeling sorry for him? And, after years of unrequited love, can Ash allow himself to hope again?

Book 5: At Last

Last year, Gemma Aldwyn roped her four best friends into making a New Year's resolution—to make the first move on potential happily-ever-after guys and break their run of being dateless for five New Year's Eves in a row. With time fast running out, Gemma is yet to find a man to kiss when the clock strikes twelve on January first. Problem is, she only wants the handsome and wealthy Greg Carmichael—Mr. Commitment-Phobic.

Greg Carmichael isn't against commitment—as long as it doesn't involve him. With beautiful women vying for his attention during his stay at one of his family's luxury resorts, Greg isn't short of female admirers. But it's his friend, Gemma Aldwyn, that he finds himself lusting after. Unfortunately, Gemma isn't into casual relationships, so sleeping with her was out of the question.

When Gemma's safety and privacy is unexpectedly threatened, she accepts the offer to hide out in the secluded Carmichael resort where Greg is staying. With this chance to get closer to Greg, can Gemma find the courage to expose her heart to great hurt? And can Greg give up his bachelor lifestyle to embrace the true gem waiting for him—before he loses her altogether?

Captured by Love Series

Book 1: The Unwilling Executive

He doesn't care about the wealth and opportunity his father offers.

Racing car mechanic Lucas Renner never expected his biological father to start acknowledging him as a son and only heir. He bet the old man has ulterior motives that has nothing to do with wanting to develop a relationship with him. He refuses to make contact with the man who has rejected him all his life... until his father's message is hand-delivered by a blushing beauty who stirs him in the right places.

She cares about keeping her job.

Jade Tully thanks her lucky stars for her new role as the personal assistant to a wealthy CEO. Heaven knows she needs it. But she doesn't anticipate getting entangled in the personal conflict between her eccentric boss and his extremely hunky son--a man who rattles her poise and melts her heart. She wants to help bring father and son together. But if she continues to do her boss's bidding, would she lose Lucas's trust and her chance to capture his heart?

Book 2: The Unyielding Bachelor

He has to stay away from her.

Thirty-year-old entrepreneur Rick Donnelly is under contract to remain unattached until his fifteen-year-old half-sister turns twenty-one. If he breaks the rules, not only will he have to hand over the management of his half-sister's substantial inheritance to his reckless stepmother, but he'll also have to transfer twenty percent ownership of his company to the untrustworthy woman. When the tempting Lexie Mead decides to knock down his heart's defenses, he finds himself in danger of breaking the contract's strict conditions--something he simply cannot afford to do.

She intends to win his heart.

Twenty-six-year-old Lexie Mead has long had feelings for the hunky Rick Donnelly. Tired of being treated as just another one of his friends, she sets out to win his heart from prettier and more aggressive women admirers. But Rick has complications to deal with... and enemies who will do anything to see him fail. She doesn't want him to lose the things he's worked hard to keep. But how can they have a future together when she is forced to walk away and Rick can't ask her to stay?

Book 3: The Undercover Playboy

He cannot let love get in the way of work.
Undercover detective Carter Garrett is required to play the role of a cash-strapped playboy to solve an important case. When Cassie Stephens, his sister's beautiful friend, starts working in the art gallery owned by a suspect, his growing feelings for her threaten to blow his cover. He mustn't let Cassie in on the secret. It could ruin his team's best chance at catching a group of criminals whose leader could very well be Cassie's new boss. But when Cassie gets embroiled in the case, his heart joins in on the action--a dangerous situation he cannot allow to persist.

Her work places her in his way.
Cassie Stephens is ecstatic to land a high-paying job with perks anyone would envy. To her further delight, her new boss has business dealings with the charming Carter Garrett, her flatmate's hunky brother. Things between her and Carter heat up with surprising speed. But being aware of Carter's playboy ways, she orders herself not to dream of a future with him... until her new boss shares a secret about Carter she wasn't at all expecting. What was more, her incredibly kind boss insists on helping her win Carter however way she can...

Book 4: The Unintended Fiancé

He arranges a fake engagement to win against his business rival.

Bradley Mead has one overriding goal: to succeed over his fiercest business enemy. To boost his chances of winning a lucrative contract over his competitor, he must first assure his potential client that he is not after the client's new wife--a woman he used to date and who still loves to flirt with him. To aid his cause, he asks Erin Baker, his sister's beautiful best friend, to be his pretend fianceé. But Erin soon becomes a pawn for his archrival's underhanded tactics... and he finds himself torn between winning in business and following the dictates of his heart.

She doesn't expect to fall for her fake fiancé.

Erin Baker believes she is now immune from Bradley Mead's charms. After all, her secret crush for him when she was still a teenager is long gone. When an ex-boyfriend becomes a new work colleague and starts annoying her, accepting Brad's proposition to be his fake fianceé for a short time seems like a great idea... until she discovers that she's been lying to herself about her feelings for him. Can she ever win the heart of the man who has never loved her back, and shows no intention of ever doing so?

Book 5: The Unforgettable Ex

He breaks the heart of the woman he loves to keep her safe.

Private detective Gavin Redford has a very dangerous enemy intent on revenge. When that criminal threatens the life of any woman he falls in love with, he has no choice but to break up with Natasha Garrett—his best friend's sister and the woman who means the world to him. No question about it, he'd rather lose her than put her in danger. But he hopes with all his heart that the thug is caught soon, because it's killing him to watch Natasha move on.

She's determined to forget the man who rejected her.

Natasha Garrett has only ever been in love once—with her brother's best friend. Unfortunately, Gavin Redford has decided he doesn't want her after all. So she will move on and forget about him. Even if her heart and body still yearns for him. Even if her mind cannot stop thinking about him. Because what choice does she have? She cannot make Gavin give his heart to her... or can she?

Book 6: The Unknown Billionaire

Will his billion-dollar fortune cause him to lose the woman he loves?
Jarryd Westbourne is shocked to have inherited a billion-dollar fortune from the mother who'd given him up for adoption. Unfortunately, business complications force him to keep it a secret from everyone for a period of time, even from Marilyn Grant, the woman he's crazy about. When his birth mother's husband suddenly challenges the will and accuses him of foul play, he ends his relationship with Marilyn to protect her from any scandal. But can he ever win Marilyn back if she discovers what he's been hiding from her?

Can her love survive a necessary deception?
Marilyn Grant was heartbroken when Jarryd Westbourne dumped her unexpectedly. But she believes that Jarryd broke up with her only because he's intimidated by her parents being billionaires while he's only of average means. She's keen to prove to Jarryd that she doesn't care one bit that his wealth is nowhere near her family's. After all, love and trust, not money, are the foundations of a lasting relationship. And Jarryd is one guy she knows she can trust…

Book 7: The Unmasked CEO

Coming soon!